BATTLEFIELD MARS

DAVID ROBBINS

BATTLEFIELD MARS

ISBN: 978-1-925342-88-8

ENTITIES UNKOWN

1

Ten-year old Piotr Zabinski was almost to the airlock when his mother said, "Hold it right there." She came over, knelt, and inspected his EVA suit.

"I want to go out," Piotr told her, fidgeting.

"Hold still." She checked the readout, and nodded. "Everything looks to be in order."

"I know how to suit up, Mom. I'm not five anymore."

She smiled and kissed him on the cheek, even though she had to know he couldn't feel it through the faceplate. "You're growing up much too fast. It seems only yesterday I was pushing you in your stroller."

"Mom," Piotr said impatiently.

"All right." She stood and tapped the code for the airlock. "What are the rules?"

Piotr sighed.

"The rules," she said again.

"Watch my air. Watch out for sharp objects. Watch the sky. Come right back in if the alarm goes off," Piotr recited.

"What else?"

Piotr had forgotten the last one. "Don't go too near the fence."

"Because?"

"Can I please just go?"

"Because?" his mother said in that irritating way she had.

Piotr hated being treated as if he were dumb. "Because if I touch it, it will short out my suit."

She raised her thumb to the pad, a green light glowed, and the inner pressure door hissed open. "Off you go. Have fun."

Piotr went through the ritual of waiting for the inner door to close and the outer door to open, and at last he was outside. He gazed up at the orange-red sky, then at the barren expanse beyond the fence, which wasn't really a fence at all but a series of poles that projected an invisible barrier.

Piotr never understood why they needed it. There wasn't any life on Mars, other than the people from Earth. Yet settlers who lived outside the New Meridian dome were required to put a fence up.

Piotr began a circuit of their house module, looking for something to stir his interest. To the north reared Albor Tholus, an extinct volcano. Ever since he first set eyes on it, he'd wanted to go there to explore. One day, his dad had promised, they would.

The rest of the scenery consisted of rocky ridges, scattered boulders, and a plain. He's seen it a thousand times. Nothing ever changed. Just all that rock and dirt, with no vegetation, no water. Compared to Earth, Mars was boring.

Grinning to himself, Piotr picked up a small stone and threw it at the security fence. It was against his mother's many rules but the stone wasn't big enough to set off the alarm, and he liked the crackle effect.

Piotr debated going to the agripod and down into the horticulture farm to watch his father work. Instead, he drifted toward the fence. He was halfway there when he happened to glance down, and stopped in surprise.

There were marks all over the dirt. Puzzled, he squatted and examined them. Each was the same. About half as wide as his hand, with a lot of small points around the edges, as there would be if his mom poked her knitting needles into the dirt.

Piotr wondered what made them. It didn't occur to him they might be tracks until he realized a trail led toward the fence. He followed it, and was dumfounded to see a hole where there had never been a hole before, rimmed by freshly dug Martian earth.

It dawned on Piotr that something must have come up out of the ground, roamed around, and gone back down again.

Piotr grew excited. His mother and father never told him about anything like this. He started to turn toward the agripod to go let his dad know but the hole piqued his curiosity.

About the size of a tractor wheel, the opening went in at an angle. Piotr couldn't see much. Kneeling, he placed his hands flat, and peered in. He heard a slight sound, and something moved. Before he could do more than gape in amazement, the thing was out of the hole—and on him.

2

Captain Archard Rahn smothered a yawn. If there was any work more boring than filing his daily report, he had yet to come across it. He glanced at the clock and saw it was only ten a.m. He needed to come up with something interesting to do for the afternoon.

Leaning back in his chair, Archard stretched. On the wall to his left hung the United Nations Interplanetary Corps banner. On the wall to his right was a map of Mars that showed the east and west hemispheres in bas relief. Near the door hung a large image, taken from space, of a bright blue pearl in the dark abyss of space

"Mother Earth," Archard said aloud. God, how he missed her. Missed being able to go outdoors without a suit. Missed being able to breathe actual fresh air. True, New Meridian's dome enabled people to do both, but only under its protective shell. And the air was artificial, supplied by the oxygenator and other components of the Atmosphere Center.

His desk phone chirped and he answered.

"Captain, this is Levlin Winslow."

Archard sat up. It was rare for the Chief Administrator to ring him up. "Sir?"

"I'm sorry to bother you," the C.A. said, sounding slightly embarrassed that he had. "It's probably nothing."

"Sir?" Archard said again. As head of security, it was his job to protect the colonists and maintain the peace. Neither required much effort, principally because there was nothing to protect the colonists from. Mars was lifeless. In the century and a half since the first colony was established, not a single indigenous life form had been discovered. As for lawbreakers, crime was as nonexistent as alien life. Not surprising, since every colonist went through a rigorous screening process. Those with sociopathic and/or psychopathic tendencies didn't make the cut. Mars would never have its very own version of Jack the Ripper.

"Do you know the Zabinski's?"

Archard brought up the personnel file on his screen, typed the name, and recited, "Family of three. Husband, Josep. Wife's name is Ania. Occupation, farmers. One child, a boy, Piotr."

"You've met them, then?"

Given the size of the colony, one hundred and twenty-one souls, Archard knew many of the people by sight if not by name. In this instance, "I went out to their farm when they first moved in to make sure their fence was up, as required. Small place. Two or three modules, the house and some sheds. Underground hydroponics. The usual."

"Well, the mother called here about, oh, an hour ago, saying their boy had disappeared—"

"Disappeared?" Archard interrupted, suddenly all interest.

"The kid went out to play, apparently. A while later the father came in and asked the mother where the boy was, and she didn't know. They both went looking and couldn't find him so the mother buzzed my office." Winslow paused. "My assistant took all this down."

"Why did they call you and not the Security Center?"

"Probably because I'm the head of the colony, and the colonists all look up to me and respect me."

Archard let that pass.

"At any rate, I wasn't in. My assistant told them I would return their call as soon as soon as I got back. Which I just did a few minutes ago."

"And?" Archard prompted when Winslow didn't go on.

"No answer. Could be they're still out looking."

Archard frowned. Military EVA suits all had comm-links. Civilian suits weren't required to; an oversight, in his judgment. But then, except for farmers and geologists and the like, few colonists ever ventured out into the real Martian environment.

"Was their fence down when the boy went missing?" Archard wondered. Sometimes a fence had to be shut off for maintenance or what-have-you, and if that was the case, the boy might have wandered off.

"The mother didn't mention anything about that," Winslow said. "Anyway, I have to go. Council meeting. Will you check this out and report back to me at your earliest convenience?"

"Of course." Archard was willing to bet a month's pay that it was nothing. Kids would be kids. Even on Mars. Still, it was something to do besides paperwork. He saved his daily report to finish later, and turned to the communications console. "Heads up, people. Where is everyone?"

"Sergeant McNee here, sir. I'm in the armory."

"Private Pasco, sir. The sarge has me mopping floors."

"Private Everett. Target range."

"Gear up, men," Archard commanded. "We're taking the tank out."

"Some action, at last," Pasco said excitedly.

"Don't get your hopes up, buddy," Private Everett said. "It's not like we'll get to shoot anything."

3

Ania Zabinski was beside herself with worry. She and her husband had searched their entire farm from top to bottom and hadn't found Piotr. Now, leaning against a corner of their house, she panted as much from fear as the running around they had been doing.

"Stay calm, will you?" Josep said. "The boy has to be somewhere."

Ania didn't care for his tone. "Of *course* he has to be somewhere."

Josep scratched his helmet as if it were his chin. "This makes no sense. The fence is working. The boy has to be in one of the buildings."

"Or lying out behind a boulder," Ania said. The terrain around the house was flat and open, but to the north, in the direction of the volcano, it was broken and rocky.

"The boy wouldn't go that far," Josep said. "He knows the rules."

"Then where?" Ania nearly wailed. She was close to tears. It was her fault they couldn't find him. She'd let Piotr go outside unsupervised, which wasn't an issue in itself. But then she had become busy with her analysis of the chemical effects of a new fertilizer they were experimenting with, and lost track of time.

Josep rubbed at his helmet. "We search again. Don't worry. Help is on its way from the colony."

"I hope they come quickly."

"We'll try the agripod again," Josep suggested.

It made sense to Ania. They'd been down there once and shouted Piotr's name but hadn't gotten an answer. Now they would search the acres and acres of plants. Nodding, she followed her hulk of a husband, taking two strides to each of his.

As was his wont, Josep thought aloud as they went. "The boy wouldn't stray off. He knows better. He wouldn't have tried to go through the fence. He knows it would damage his suit. He wasn't in the sheds. He has to be underground, in the fields."

Ania recalled that back on Earth, fields were always on the surface. Yet another of the many differences between their own planet and this red one. "Could he have taken a tool and hurt himself?"

"Unlikely. The boy wouldn't take one without permission. But I'll check when we get down there, just the same."

"Maybe he fell and hit his head on a seeding tray or a bin."

"Stop your fretting. He was wearing his helmet. It would protect him."

"He might have opened it. The fields are pressurized," Ania reminded him. The artificial atmosphere was as close to Earth's as possible.

Josep unexpectedly stopped and pointed. "Look. More of those strange marks."

Ania didn't care about stupid circles in the dirt. She would try to figure them out later. Right now all she cared about was their son.

The agripod airlock was larger than most to accommodate some of the equipment they used. A flight of stairs led down.

Before them spread the glory of their farm; wheat and oats, corn and potatoes, and more. The corn stalks were the highest.

Ania decided that was where she would look and took a step, only to have Josep grab her wrist.

"What in God's name?"

Ania's blood went cold.

Not two meters from the stairwell, a wall that should be solid had a dark hole, maybe a meter across, in the center.

"What could have caused that?" Josep said, sounding dazed. He went toward it.

Ania was more bothered by deep scratches in the wall below the hole. "What are those?"

"Eh?" Josep bent, then caught himself and pointed off across their fields. "Look! The corn! It's moving!"

Sure enough, the stalks were swaying as if to a mild breeze.

Ania put a hand to her throat. "Piotr!" Certain it must be their son, she raced down the center aisle. Josep called her name but she didn't stop. All that mattered was Piotr. She flew past waist-high wheat and then the oats. Josep uttered another cry, not her name but something she didn't catch. "I must find Piotr!" she shouted into her mic.

The corn stopped moving.

"Piotr?" Ania called. She parted the stalks and peered along the rows but didn't see him. "Son, where are you?"

Only then did Ania notice another hole at the far end of the horticultural habitat. "Josep. Come here. Hurry."

When there was no answer, Ania turned.

Her husband was nowhere to be seen.

"Josep?" Ania started back.

A profound stillness prevailed.

An uneasy feeling came over her. She tried to swallow but her mouth was dry. Licking her lips, she shouted, "Josep? Where are you?"

Ania was almost past the wheat plot when she realized that stalks out in the middle were moving. Specifically, several swaths were bending in her direction.

"Josep!" Ania yelled, scared. She ran until the stairs were in view. So was a figure sprawled on the floor, and the strange things swarming over it. Sheer horror brought her lurching to a stop.

Hideous creatures were ripping her husband to pieces. Already they had torn through his EVA suit, his clothes, his flesh. Blood was everywhere. Worse, one of his attackers was pulling his intestines out of his abdomen. Another raised Josep's dripping heart aloft.

Ania nearly swooned. She stumbled, regained her footing, and turned to flee. She would hide until the things were gone and report them to…

Several more had come out of the wheat and were scuttling toward her.

Ania screamed. She was still screaming when one of the creatures launched itself at her, still screaming when one of its limbs speared through her suit into her throat. Her scream became a gurgle.

Then more of them were on her.

4

The 'tank' was a rover constructed to military specs. Armor-plated with a synthetic harder than the titanium of yesteryear, yet barely a third of the weight, its main armament consisted of a DEW array on top. Directed Energy Weapon systems varied. In this instance, the powers-that-be had decided all three tanks on Mars—one at each of the colonies—should have masers.

A decision Archard didn't agree with. Microwaves were lethal but give him a laser any day. Quicker to power up, they sliced through anything and everything.

Standing beside the tank's open bay, he waited for his men to file out of the ready room. He heard their voices, and turned, catching sight of his reflection on the mirror-surface wall.

His EVA suit was standard military issue, no different from those of his men except for the officer's bars on his shoulders. It occurred to him how glad they should be that their streamlined suits had replaced the bulky outfits of the early space age. He'd read that getting around in those had been a chore.

A breakthrough in nanotech made it possible. Virtually a second skin, they fit as snugly as clothes.

Oversized helmets were a thing of the past, too. For the U.N.I.C, anyway. Theirs fit like a skull cap. All they had to do was press a stud and the flexi-glass faceplate extended to form a seal with the main suit.

With his crew-cut blond hair and blue eyes, his Individual Combat Weapon and his web belt and sidearm, Archard couldn't help reflecting that he looked like a poster boy for the Interplanetary Corps.

"Hop to it!" a gruff voice barked, and into the motor pool strode Sergeant McNee. From the East End of London, everything about the man screamed career military, from his buzz cut to his crisp uniform. Snapping to attention, he saluted, then turned and growled in his clipped British accent, "On the double. We don't want to keep the captain waiting."

Privates Everett and Pasco were still putting themselves together. Everett, who hailed from Kentucky, had been in the Corps five years now. Pasco, from Seville, Spain, was barely six months out of basic; he tried hard but bumbled and fumbled at nearly everything he did. His ICW wasn't slung, and he nearly tripped over the strap.

"Get your act together, soldier," Sergeant McNee said.

"Yes, sir," Pasco said, then almost tripped a second time.

Yet another thing Archard didn't understand was why the higher-ups sent a kid like Pasco to Mars. The entire planet was one giant inhospitable environment, with no mercy for the careless.

Archard stepped aside so his men could enter the tank.

"You mentioned a missing person, sir?" Sergeant McNee said.

"A ten-year-old boy."

"Could be serious then?"

Archard knew what the non-com was thinking. They might actually get to do something useful for once instead of sitting on their asses cleaning weapons that never saw use. "Let's hope not."

"Sir?" McNee said, then blinked. "Not that I'd wish any harm to come to the tyke."

Private Pasco had taken his seat and was adjusting the seatbelt. "I bet he's fine, Sarge. I got lost a lot when I was a kid, and I'm still here."

A look of annoyance came over McNee and he opened his mouth to reply but Archard shook his head and motioned him forward. "Systems check, if you would. Private Everett, seal the bay door." He made for the front passenger seat. "I want us underway ASAP."

"Look out, Mars," Private Pasco said. "Here we come."

5

Archard had once heard the Martian landscape described as 'spectacular,' and as 'vistas of pure wonder.' But the people who made those claims, he'd noticed, had never been there.

Mars was pretty much a cold, barren wasteland. There were mountains and valleys and plains, but without a speck of life anywhere.

Even the outlying farms were bare of life. The growing took place in underground habitats. There weren't any tiled fields, no rose gardens, no trees.

The Zabinski farm was typical. From a distance, it was as unremarkable as the ground it stood on. There was a standard house module, prefabricated in sections on Earth, and a couple of sheds. Plus the agripod that led down to the growing area.

Sergeant McNee activated a screen on the dash, and frowned. "No sign of anyone, sir. No heat signatures anywhere."

"Where can they be?" Archard had been trying to raise the family the whole ride out. That they weren't responding didn't overly worry him. They might be down in the horticulture habitat, which could interfere with reception.

"You'd think they would be waiting for us," Private Everett remarked.

"I hope their kid is okay," Private Pasco said.

Sergeant McNee let out an oath and braked sharply without being ordered to.

"Why did you stop?" Archard demanded.

"Are those *holes*?"

The tank was winding down a grade to the homestead. Below, the terrain was essentially flat for a good distance.

"I don't see..." Archard began.

"The house, sir," Sergeant McNee said. "Get a load of the house."

Domicile Modules, as they were called, were well-nigh indestructible. They had to be, to resist decompression. An ICW could punch a hole in one with a 20mm High Explosive round, but not much else could make a dent. Yet to Archard's amazement, there were several holes in the side of the house. Fairly large, too.

Private Pasco gasped. "If anyone was inside when that happened..." He didn't finish.

"Get going," Archard said to McNee.

"Should I man the maser, sir?" Private Everett asked, with a bob of his chin at the bubble above the bay.

"No need for that," Archard said. The maser was for use against enemies in combat, and on the Red Planet, humans didn't have any enemies.

The ring of power poles that formed the security fence appeared intact. Blinking lights on the poles on either side of the dirt road that led into the farm warned the fence was active.

"Helmets," Archard said, and sealed his. Unbuckling his safety harness, he moved to the airlock. "Is everyone reading me?"

"Affirmative," Sergeant McNee replied.

"Clear as a bell, sir," Everett said.

"Yep," Pasco said.

"That will be 'yes, sir,' mister, or I'll have you on report," Sergeant McNee snapped.

"Yes, sir!"

"Everett, you're with me," Archard said. "Sergeant, keep monitoring. If you pick up their heat signatures, let me know immediately." Opening the inner door, he stepped in, waited for the pressure to equalize, then opened the outer. It was annoying to have to go through the procedure every time, but otherwise the vehicle would decompress, with disastrous results.

Hefting his weapon, Archard waited for Everett. He happened to glance toward the distant volcano and spied a large shape silhouetted against the Martian sky.

And it was moving.

6

Archard quickly increased the magnification on his helmet display while zooming in on the exact spot. All he saw was bare crater rim. A trick of light and shadow, he decided.

Private Everett had emerged, his weapon at the ready. Never much of a talker—unlike Pasco, who could talk rings around a tree—Everett was the best marksman in their unit. He even outshot Sergeant McNee.

Archard went to the 'gate,' which wasn't any such thing in the conventional sense. It merely meant the power poles to either side were spaced further apart to allow vehicles through. He could hear their slight hum.

A little known fact; sounds on Mars didn't travel as far as they did on Earth. The atmosphere was so thin, a blast from his ICW would only be heard a hundred meters away.

Archard had long been puzzled by the government's requirement that every settler erect a security fence. What did the settlers need one for when there wasn't anything on Mars that could harm them?

Thankfully, in case of emergencies, the U.N.I.C. could shut any fence down with an override code. Archard entered it into the access panel. The LED lights on the posts dimmed, and he walked through. "Take point."

"Sir," Private Everett acknowledged, and hurried past.

"Sergeant McNee," Archard said, "let us get forty meters in, then bring the tank. Sensors at max."

"Understood."

Private Everett's faceplate was glued to his targeting scope.

"Make sure your helmet is on full spectrum sweep," Archard ordered. Usually reserved for combat situations, full sweeps included everything from infrared to ultraviolet.

"Already is, sir."

Archard took pride in always being thorough. When he went at something, he went at it one hundred percent. You could say it was his dominant trait. In fact, when he underwent the psyche profiling administered to Corps volunteers, the psychiatrist who examined him made a special mention of his 'intense focus.' It was his focus that accounted for Archard excelling at every aspect of his training. It was his focus that accounted for him being on Mars.

The wind picked up, creating little swirls of dust. Archard's helmet display registered gusts to 80 kph. On Mars that was nothing.

Private Everett abruptly stopped and lowered his ICW. He was looking down, and gave a slight start.

"What are you...?" Archard began, and saw for himself. The ground was pockmarked with dozens of peculiar impressions. He enlarged them on his helmet holo. They averaged nine centimeters in diameter, and around the edges were little points he couldn't account for.

"Call me crazy, sir," Private Everett said, and there was an unnerved quality to his voice that Archard never heard before, "but I think they're tracks."

Archard knew that Everett was from the United States, from a place called Kentucky, and that their marksman had done a lot of tracking and hunting back among the green hills of Earth. But if Everett was right, it begged an unthinkable question.

What made them?

7

More tracks were near the house, clustered under the holes.

Archard clicked his mic. "Sergeant McNee?"

"Sir?"

"Bring the tank up but don't get out. Continue full scan. Be alert for…" Archard was reluctant to say what common sense told him was obvious, "…anything anomalous."

"Anomalous, sir?" the non-com repeated.

"Out of the ordinary, Sergeant."

Settlers were required to provide the U.N.I.C. with copies of their thumb prints, which were the standard access keys. Archard brought up Josep Zabinski's on his wrist screen, held it to the airlock reader, and the outer door slid open.

"Shouldn't I go first, sir?" Everett said.

"I'm not one of those officers who leads from behind."

Entering, Archard waited as the airlock cycled, then swept inside in a crouch.

The place looked as if an Earth hurricane had hit it. Or, to be precise, explosive decompression. Furniture was shattered or upended, objects scattered, broken items everywhere.

"It's a shambles," Archard said.

Everett had followed him in and was looking around. "I don't see any bodies, sir."

Stepping over a busted chair, Archard crossed the living room to the kitchen. Cupboards had been ripped open, dishes smashed to pieces. A flour bin had burst, showering flour over everything. And there in the flour on the floor, as clear as in the dirt outside, were more of the bizarre tracks.

"We'll check the agripod next," Archard said.

"Let's hope it's not in the same shape."

Archard was through the airlock and waiting for the Kentuckian when his comm-link buzzed.

"Sir, I think I'm picking up something on the motion sensors," Sergeant McNee reported.

"You *think*?"

"It's faint. From off toward the volcano. Could it be the Zabinskis, do you think?"

Archard doubted it. "What would they be doing on Albor Tholus? Keep monitoring."

The airlock was taking forever. At moments like this, Archard missed the simple doors on Earth. Open them, go through, close them. Easy-peasy. Not on Mars. Airlocks were notoriously slow, sometimes irritatingly so, yet essential.

When Bradbury, the first colony, was established, some civilians complained. They wanted the government to come up with a better way. Then a freak glitch caused both doors to an outer airlock to open simultaneously. Eleven people lost their lives, and half a block was destroyed, before the emergency override resealed the dome. No one had complained since.

Finally, Private Everett emerged.

Archard gestured, and they spread out and approached the agripod. Once again, they had to endure an airlock.

The first thing Archard noticed on entering was the complete and utter silence. With Everett at his back, he warily descended the stairs. At the bottom, he barely had time to take in the sight of a lake of blood mixed with viscera when something flew at him from out of the shadows, screeching wildly.

8

Archard reacted instinctively. He pointed his ICW but instantly jerked his weapon down and shouted, "Hold your fire!"

"Good God," Private Everett blurted.

It was the boy, Piotr Zabinski, in a child's EVA suit, covered with blood. His features were twisted in unbridled terror the likes of which no child his age should ever experience, his wide eyes filled with the fire of near madness. But it was what the boy held that shocked Archard most. For clutched to Piotr's breast was the severed head of Ania Zabinski, his mother. Her own eyes were glazed testimony to the horror she had felt at the moment of dying. Her mouth was agape in her death scream.

"Good God," Everett said again.

It brought Archard out of his shock. "Piotr?" he said, and reached out.

The boy bounded back and shook his head, uttering inarticulate sounds.

"Piotr? Do you remember me?" Archard said. "I was here once. I'm Captain Rahn. U.N.I.C. I had coffee with your father and mother? Do you remember?"

"Mom," the boy said softly, and gave a violent shake. He looked at the grisly head, tears trickling down his cheeks. "They...they tore her apart, like they did Dad. They..."

"We're here to help," Archard said soothingly. "I can take that from you if you want."

"No!" Piotr cried, and clutched the head tight. Sniffling, he said in a barely audible whisper, "They didn't tear me apart. That one, it just...it just..." He quaked some more.

Archard waited. To try and pick the boy up would only aggravate matters.

"Sir, did you see this?" Private Everett said. "What the hell? I mean, *what the hell?*"

Keeping one eye on the boy, Archard half-turned. The remains of the parents were about ten meters apart. Their arms and legs had been torn off and placed on either side of their bodies. Internal organs had been ripped out and piled in the cavities. Everything had been removed; their hearts, their gall bladders, their spleens, kidneys, livers, and more.

"What could do this?" Everett said in bewilderment.

"*They* did it," Piotr said.

Archard shifted so he blocked the boy's view. "What were they? What did you see?"

Piotr whimpered, hugged his mother's head, and said fearfully, "Monsters."

9

Archard's helmet shrilled.

"Movement, sir," Sergeant McNee reported. "No doubt about it this time. Along with faint sounds I can't identify."

"Infrared?"

"No heat signatures. How that can be, I have no idea."

"On Albor Tholus?"

"No, sir. About a hundred and fifty meters from the farm, heading toward the volcano."

A tingle of excitement rippled through Archard. He turned to the boy. "Piotr, would you like to catch the things that did this to your parents?"

"Yes," Piotr sniffled. Then, more fiercely, "Yes!"

Archard scooped him into his arms. He was tempted to try and wrest the head away but time was critical. "We're coming out," he barked into his comm-link. "Be ready to roll."

By the time they cleared the airlock, Sergeant McNee had brought the tank close to the agripod. The moment he was inside, Archard carried Piotr to the bench in the bay and set him down. "This is Private Pasco. He'll look after you for a while."

The Spaniard smiled and nodded. "Si. I mean, yes, sir, I am happy to."

Archard claimed his seat. The holograph showed ripples where the long-range sensors detected motion.

He honed in, on visual, but only saw flat ground and a few boulders. "Odd."

"Maybe they're invisible," Sergeant McNee joked.

"Let's find out."

At top acceleration, the tank could do 70 kph. It was a lot faster than civilian rovers, but for Archard it wasn't fast enough. He was eager for a glimpse of the 'monsters.'

"I couldn't believe your helmet feed of the farmer and his wife," McNee said grimly.

"The boy," Archard said quietly.

"Oh. Sorry, sir."

The tank neared the far side of the fence. Except for the 'gate' out front, the poles were a lot closer together.

"The tank is too wide to make it through," Sergeant McNee pointed out the obvious. "Do we stop and go on foot?"

"I want these things, whatever they are. The fence is off so it won't damage the tank."

"Understood," Sergeant McNee said, then called out. "Brace yourselves."

There was the mildest of jolts as the tank plowed a pole under.

Private Pasco let out a whoop.

Archard put his nose to the windshield. The sensors said there was movement so there had to be something up ahead, but for the life of him he still didn't see anything.

Sergeant McNee indicated the holo. "We're losing them."

The ripples were fading in and out.

"Faster," Archard urged.

"Too bad this thing doesn't have thrusters," McNee muttered.

The ripples blinked a few times, and were gone. Archard checked that the sensor gain was boosted all the way, and it was.

"They're gone, sir," Sergeant McNee said.

"Stop the tank. Everett, you're on me."

Once through the airlock, Archard scoured for signs of life, for more of the bizarre tracks, for anything at all.

"It's like we're chasing ghosts," Everett remarked.

"Ghosts don't tear off arms and rip out organs."

"What now, sir? Do we head back to New Meridian?"

"We do not."

"Then where, if you don't mind my asking?"

"Where do you think?" Archard rejoined, and jabbed a finger at the extinct volcano.

10

It didn't take a tactical genius to deduce that Albor Tholus must harbor the answers they needed. That large *thing* on the rim. The creatures that attacked the farm hurrying toward it after the attack.

First, though, Archard needed to warn New Meridian. He piped through to the Chief Administrator's office. Winslow's assistant balked at relaying his call, claiming the C.A. was in a meeting and couldn't be disturbed. Archard said he would count to three, and if Winslow wasn't on the line, he would take the assistant into custody when he got back for obstructing a U.N.I.C. officer in the performance of his duties.

"This is Levlin Winslow. Who is this? What is so important that—?"

"Captain Rahn," Archard cut him off. "We have trouble. I need you to listen. If you're with someone else, have them leave."

"I don't know if I like your tone, Captain," Winslow said archly.

Archard had forgotten how full of himself the man could be. "You have one minute."

"Now see here…"

"Winslow, the farmer and his wife are dead…"

"What?"

"Killed by entities unknown, we'll call them for now."

"What?"

"My unit is in pursuit." Archard paused. "Are you alone yet?" He heard muffled voices and a commotion, and the C.A. came back on.

"Run all that by me again, would you?"

"First things first. Under Article Three, Section B, Subsection N, paragraph four of the United Nations Colonization Protocols, as head of security for New Meridian I formally declare a state of emergency."

"Now wait just a damn minute."

"You are required to follow my instructions. Any breach of protocol and I'll have you brought up before a tribunal."

"Hold on, hold on. All this is going too fast."

"Catch up," Archard said. "I'll repeat this only once. Josep and Ania Zabinski are dead. We're going after the creatures that killed them." Archard thought to add, "Their boy is safe and in our custody."

"What was that about creatures?"

"That's all I can tell you for now. It's all we know."

"You can't mean *Martians*?"

"Animals, possibly, Chief Administrator," Archard said.

"The government's official policy is that Mars doesn't have indigenous life forms."

"Tell that to the couple the indigenous life killed." Archard remembered the boy was listening, and frowned at his blunder.

"Are you sure it wasn't a mishap of some kind? You might be jumping to the wrong conclusion. No one has ever reported anything like this."

"Do I have to bring you out to their farm and rub your nose in their blood?"

"No, no. That was harsh. I'll do whatever you require of me. It's just so incredible."

"Contact all the outlying settlers. Order them to New Meridian. If any refuse, tell them I'll show up personally to drag them in by the scruff of their necks."

"Goodness, you're in a mood."

"And Winslow?"

"There's more?"

"Pray that whatever attacked the farm doesn't know about New Meridian. Because if they do, and breach the dome, the colony is in serious danger."

"You're exaggerating, surely."

"I wish I were," Archard said.

Albor Tholus. Over seven kilometers high and one hundred and sixty kilometers wide. The caldera itself, from which the hot lava once spewed, was thirty kilometers across. Satellite images suggested that the main vent went deep underground. Exactly how deep no one could say since no one had ever been down there.

All this went through Archard's head as the tank wound among giant boulders and basalt outcroppings. The rugged terrain had slowed them considerably.

Time for more intel, Archard decided. Rising, he walked back to the bay and sat across from Private Pasco and Piotr Zabinski.

The boy was slumped in despair, still clutching his mother's head as if it were the most precious thing in the world.

"Piotr, we need to talk."

The child looked up. His eyes were moist, his lower lip quivering.

Archard proceeded with care. He wasn't a psychologist but he could tell Piotr was on the cusp of a breakdown. "Do you remember the time I visited your farm?"

"Yes. You had your gun."

Archard smiled. "I always have my gun. My name is Archard. I'd like…"

"What are you?" Piotr broke in.

"I beg your pardon?"

"Your country. Your people. We're Polish. My dad…" Piotr stopped, and sniffled. "My dad was proud of that. He said it's good to know where a person comes from. That you can tell a lot about them."

"I'm German."

Piotr's brow furrowed. "My dad said Germans like to make things like cars and rockets. He said they are good soldiers."

"Here I sit," Archard said.

The boy gnawed his lip, thinking. "From my studies…the countries are very close, yes?"

"Germany and Poland? They're next to each other. We're neighbors, you might say."

"Ah." Piotr almost smiled.

"I need your help," Archard eased into it.

"Me? What can I do?"

"My men and I are after the things that hurt your parents. We want to punish them for what they did."

A savage gleam came into the boy's eyes. "Kill them all."

Archard rested his elbows on his knees. "It would help us greatly if we knew what we are up against."

"Monsters."

"You said that before. But what *kind* of monsters, Piotr? What are they like? What can you tell me about them that might help us?"

"They're scary."

"I need more than that. What do they look like? How big are they? How fast do they move? Those sorts of things."

"Oh."

"Please, Piotr. A soldier must learn all he can about an enemy. Their weaknesses. Their strengths. What they do."

"The first one," Piotr began, and trembled. "The first one came out of a hole and jumped on me. I was so scared I fell on my back. It stood over me on its long legs—"

"How many legs?"

Piotr removed his left arm from his mother's head and held up his fingers one by one, counting. "Eight. If you don't count the grippers."

"The what?"

"It's how they hold stuff. How they tear..." Piotr trembled. "How they tear people apart."

"All right. What did it do then?"

"It looked at me for the longest while with its awful eyes." Piotr closed his, and when he went on, he did so in a mechanical tone. "They move all around. One can go up while the other goes down."

"What moves? Their eyes?"

Piotr's helmet bobbed. "Their eyes aren't in their heads, like ours. They're at the ends of wavy things."

Archard tried to picture it. "What do you mean by wavy things?"

Before the boy could reply, Sergeant McNee shouted, "Sir! There's something up ahead that you should see."

11

The tank was approaching the base of Albor Tholus, the slope seeming to rise forever. Hundreds of meters up, a flurry of dust rose from some sort of disturbance.

Sergeant McNee braked and boosted the amplification on the holo to no avail. "Can't tell what that is. Pressure escaping, maybe?"

Archard deemed that unlikely. According to the experts, the volcano had gone inactive millions of years ago.

"I thought I saw something when I first noticed the dust," the non-com said.

"Be more specific."

"I can't. It was moving, that's all I could tell. But now there's no sign of the bloody thing."

The red dust was settling and thinning. Another minute, and all that was left were wisps.

"Heads up, everyone," Archard said, and pointed at the volcano.

Sergeant McNee took the hint and continued on. "I hate slopes like this."

So did Archard; they were treacherous in the extreme. Ground that appeared solid might give way without warning.

"Sir, I've been thinking," McNee said. "Shouldn't we contact Wellsville and Bradbury? Major Howard and Colonel Vasin will want to know about the attack, won't they?"

Wellsville and Bradbury were the second and first colonies, respectively. Green and Vasin were the heads of their U.N.I.C. details.

"When I have something concrete to report, I will," Archard said.

Presently, they came to where the dust cloud had been raised. Exiting the airlock, Archard roved for sign. He only went a couple of steps, and there, imprinted in the soil, were more strange marks exactly like those at the farm, only larger. They ringed a disturbed area about three meters across. At its center was a depression of loose dirt.

Archard had the impression that the ground had been scooped out and resettled again. Gingerly placing his foot in the disturbed area, he slowly applied his full weight. It didn't give way. Sinking to his knees, he scraped with his fingers. Some of the dirt trickled inward, but that was all.

Archard returned to the tank. Private Pasco was trying to persuade Piotr to hand over his mother's head but the boy was shaking his and saying, "No! No! You can't have her!"

Archard intervened, asking nicely, "How about if you give her to me, Piotr? I'll wrap her in a blanket to keep her safe."

"They might take it like they did my dad's," Piotr said tearfully.

"Was that at the agripod?"

Piotr nodded. "After that first monster looked at me a while, it went back down the hole. I was so afraid, I ran to a shed and hid there I don't know how long. When the monster didn't come after me, I ran to the agripod to tell my dad but didn't see him. I heard a noise and saw what I thought was the same monster coming through the wall so I hid in the potato patch." Piotr talked faster. "A whole lot of those things came out. I figured they were hunting me. That was when dad and mom showed up. I should have yelled to warn them but all I did was lie there, I was so scared." He stopped, and sobbed. "Everything happened so fast. The monsters tore my dad apart, and then they went after mom."

"You don't need to go on," Archard said, but Piotr didn't seem to hear him.

"One of them would hold up part of my dad or mom, and the others would look at it. My dad's head they looked at the longest, until the one holding it went into the hole."

Archard was going to ask how the boy got his hands on his mother's head when Sergeant McNee let out with an excited, "Captain! We might have found where those things come from."

"Enlighten me," Archard said.

"Sensors show a cave."

12

Caves were common on Mars but few had been explored. It was too dangerous. One slip, one fall, and an EVA suit could be punctured. Plus, the government had made it illegal to venture into a cave without official approval. There were forms that must be submitted. Few requests were ever made. The colonists had better things to do than bumble around in subterranean death traps.

Sergeant McNee brought the tank to a halt on a basalt shelf.

Before them gaped a black hole that the Red Planet's weak sunlight failed to penetrate. Rimmed by sharp projections much like teeth, it gave Archard the impression of staring into the gullet of a gigantic beast. He issued orders. Everyone was to refill their EVA suit air supply from the reservoir in the tank. They were to recheck their weapons. Batteries should be at full strength, or replaced. Spare bulbs for their spotlights, as well as coils of rope, and bolts, were also essential. He left nothing to chance.

"Private Pasco, you'll stay with the vehicle and keep Piotr company. Under no circumstances is he to venture outside."

"Yes, sir," Pasco said, unable to hide his disappointment that he wasn't going with them.

"Sit up front and monitor us. If we lose contact or our vitals flat line, you're to proceed immediately to New Meridian. On the way, raise Wellsville by satellite. It's closest, and you shouldn't have any trouble getting through unless there's a sandstorm. Inform Captain Howard of developments. He'll take it from there."

Archard had Private Everett fill a bag with flares and instructed Sergeant McNee to bring two dozen locator beacons from the equipment locker. No bigger than a thumbnail, they could broadcast a signal for up to a month before they drained dry.

The wind had died. As they approached the dark maw, the only sound was the tread of their boots and the barely noticeable rasp of their breathers.

The cave mouth was five meters across and about twice that high. Beyond, their spotlights revealed an ancient lava tube, angling down.

With Sergeant McNee flanking right and Private Everett flanking left, Archard entered. They hadn't gone a dozen steps when McNee pointed at the wall and said, "Sir."

Scratch marks, a lot of them, just like at the Zabinski farm.

"No life on Mars, my ass," Private Everett said.

Archard, too, had been wondering how the experts could be so wrong. Centuries had gone by since the first NASA rover roamed the Red Planet, yet the scientists were clueless. Or were they? A troubling notion occurred to him. The ban on unauthorized cave exploration, the edict about perimeter fences. Did the government know more than it let on? Would the powers-that-be keep such a terrible secret from the colonists? Surely not, he told himself.

"Nothing on sensors yet, sir," Everett said.

"A thought, Captain, if I may," Sergeant McNee said.

"I'm listening."

"We *know* there are creatures of some kind. We know they headed here from the farm. Yet we didn't pick up their heat signatures. We didn't pick up hardly anything at all." The non-com gazed worriedly down the tube. "What if we *can't* read them? We'll be going in blind."

"We have eyes. We have ears." Archard moved on, knowing full well McNee had a valid point. It could be none of them would make it out alive.

13

The lava tube was like a giant vein, blood-red with streaks of black, the basalt reflecting their spotlights with bright intensity.

Gradually, the passage narrowed. They could no longer walk abreast.

Archard assumed the lead. His helmet display continued to read negative although once he thought there was a flicker of motion from deeper in.

Every two hundred meters, Sergeant McNee affixed a locator to the tunnel wall.

Every quarter-hour, Archard radioed the tank. Pasco reported all was well. The third check, Pasco let him know Piotr had fallen asleep cradling his mother's head.

"Do you want me to try and take it away from him, sir?"

"You couldn't without waking him, and he'd be upset," Archard said. "Leave him be. He's been through enough."

"It's so weird, him holding onto that thing."

"If it was all you had left of your mother, you might do the same. Now hush up. I want complete comm silence unless I say otherwise."

The farther they descended, the more scratches they came across. Not just on the sides and the bottom but the top as well, suggesting that whatever the creatures were, they could cling upside down to a surface as hard as metal and as smooth as glass.

The tube curved.

Archard held his left fist up, signaling a halt. He cautiously crept forward and peered around. The tunnel appeared empty. He signaled for McNee and Everett to follow, and advanced. He was looking ahead, not at the ground, and when something crunched under his foot, he glanced down. With an oath, he recoiled, jerking the ICW to his shoulder.

"Sir?" Sergeant McNee was instantly at his side.

"A dead one, by God," Private Everett said.

That it was. Long dead, and desiccated. Only part of it remained, a couple of legs attached to a round piece about forty centimeters across.

"Can't tell much from that," McNee said.

Archard slid his fingers under a leg and tried to raise it. Light as a feather, it dissolved into pieces. He lightly touched the rounded section, and where he touched dissolved away, too.

"At least we know they can die," Private Everett said.

They passed smaller tubes that branched off. They came to junctions and always chose whichever tube seemed to lead deeper into the bowels of the volcano. By now, Archard estimated, they must be a kilometer under the surface.

Yet another curve was bathed in their beams. At the same instant, Archard's motion sensor went off. He stopped and boosted his audio input so high that if he sneezed, he'd hurt his eardrums. Odd sounds filtered in. Tapping, was how he'd describe it. A burst, then silence, then another burst.

"What in the world?" Private Everett whispered.

Archard could have slugged him. He scowled, and Sergeant McNee slapped Everett on the arm.

With a finger to his helmet, Archard edged to the bend. He had no idea what he would see. He thought he was ready for anything. The U.N.I.C. had exhaustively trained him to compartmentalize and contain his emotions. It didn't always work, though, like back at the farm when he saw the slaughter.

And now.

Reality as Archard knew it crumbled, and nightmare became real.

14

The tube ended in a cavern that stretched so far and so high that the other side was lost in the distance, a cavern that sank down and down and down even more, until there didn't seem to be a bottom.

The sheer immensity staggered Archard's senses. Yet the cavern paled compared to the things that filled it. Literally, it crawled with life.

Archard had expected to find fauna of some kind, animal life, albeit alien, at least by Earth standards. He didn't expect to find highly intelligent life. He didn't expect to find an entire civilization.

Before his amazed gaze unfolded a bustling, thriving, underground city, although 'city' didn't apply in an Earth-sense. There were no skyscrapers, no suburbs, no streets, few comparable frames of reference.

There were ramps and walkways and wider avenues, all composed of basalt, crisscrossing one above another, traversing spans of hundreds of meters.

There were structures, obelisks and spires and spheres and triangles and pentagons, and shapes the human mind had never conceived, on cliffs and mesas and broad shelves.

There were life forms, a multitude of living organisms, moving ceaselessly to and fro, up the ramps and along the thoroughfares and going in and out of the structures. Some were small, some large. Multi-legged, one and all.

Archard blinked, shook his helmet, and looked again. It wasn't a hallucination induced by a suit leak or his tank air gone foul. Yet his sensors, even this close, failed to register any heat signatures. The sensors did pick up motion, but weakly, as the sensors had in the tank.

He focused on the life forms and made out different types. The majority—he would estimate seventy percent—possessed circular bodies about a meter round. Pinkish-red, they were covered by a carapace or shell that rose slightly in the center, and supported by eight legs about half a meter long. Two appendages projected from the 'front,' each ending in several long 'grippers,' as Piotr had called them. Then there were their eyes, attached at the end of thin stalks that constantly moved up and down and from side to side, just as the boy said.

Of the several kinds of larger beings, the one Archard could make out the best was traveling along an elevated walkway not far off. Nine meters in length, it, too, had eight legs, and grippers, but an elongated body with a bulky blue carapace that tapered into a segmented tail.

Archard was so intent on the spectacle that he almost didn't catch the movement near his feet. Glancing down, he was startled to find one of the smaller creatures with its stalk eyes fixed on him. Even as he saw it, the thing extended its grippers toward his faceplate.

Archard sprang back and jammed the ICW'S stock to his shoulder, but the thing didn't attack. It stood perfectly still except for its eyes, which reminded Archard of a photo he'd seen as a boy of an assassin fly. He remembered it because at the time its name had struck him as cool; an *assassin* fly. He also remembered how fascinated he had been by its multifaceted compound eyes.

The creature appeared to be studying him. Its stalks roved up and down, from his boots to his helmet.

Archard didn't shoot. The thing wasn't acting hostile, merely curious. The grippers, he now saw, were three long digits, or 'fingers,' the middle one thicker than the other two.

Archard had another reason for not shooting. His squad was hopelessly outnumbered. He'd much rather back away without provoking the thing, get to the surface, and contact New Meridian. The colony, every colony, must be alerted.

He glanced past the creature, and the short hairs at the nape of his neck prickled.

Nearly all activity in the cavern had ceased. Every last Martian had stopped and swung their eye stalks in his direction.

A chill swept through Archard. The implications were staggering. He backpedaled, but the moment he moved, so did the creature. The thing came at him in a scrambling rush, its legs clacking on the basalt like sticks on rock.

Archard fired. He had the selector set to single shot, and he sent a slug into the creature's round body. At the blast, the thing jerked, and kept coming. Archard had no time to dwell on why the armor-piercing round hadn't brought it down. He flipped the selector switch to semi-auto and triggered a three-round burst. The creature partially buckled but came on again. It was almost on him, its grippers centimeters from his face, when Archard flicked to full auto and emptied half his magazine.

The thing shuddered and collapsed.

Out in the cavern, the Martians were waving their stalks and their front limbs in what might be a frenzy of rage. Fortunately, none of the walkways connected to the tube. That wouldn't stop them, though; not when they could scale sheer walls.

Wheeling, Archard bounded around the bend and almost collided with Sergeant McNee and Private Everett, who were rushing to his aid. "Run!" he shouted. When the non-com went to say something, he pushed him and bawled, "Don't talk! Just run! Run for your lives!"

In bulky civilian EVA suits, running was a chore. Thanks to the military's streamlined versions, and Mars' lesser gravity, troopers could run as fast as they could on Earth for short distances. Still, it took a lot out of them. Archard was puffing after a hundred meters, and sweating profusely after two hundred, even though he worked out every day; rigorous exercise was required to prevent muscular entropy.

Archard twisted at the waist to look back. Once again his sensors failed to show heat signatures. But the display read motion, and no wonder.

A dozen of the things were after them.

15

Another ten meters, and Archard whirled. "Behind us!" he bellowed. He'd like to use a frag but the creatures were too close. While his suit could automatically seal small punctures, he didn't dare take the risk of something worse.

Archard cut loose. The foremost creature fell, heaved up, managed several more steps, and pitched forward for good.

Those behind it leaped over its body.

Sergeant McNee and Private Everett unleashed 5.56mm hailstorms, dropping more.

Archard raked one in midair and it flipped and thrashed wildly, its legs reaching for him even in its death throes.

The last of the things ran into a withering blast from McNee. Riddled, it scuttled another meter and was almost at Archard's feet when it went still.

"Damn!" Private Everett exclaimed.

"Keep going," Archard said, certain more would come. He reloaded as he went.

"What *are* they?" Everett said.

McNee, more tactical minded, asked, "How many are we up against?"

"I don't know how many will come after us, but I saw thousands," Archard related. He concentrated on pacing himself, on his breathing, on putting as much distance as he could between them and the Martians.

Martians. It felt strange to even think the word. All those early expeditions. Almost two centuries of colonization. And no one knew. It seemed impossible. And yet, if the Martians lived underground and seldom came to the surface, the odds of encountering them were next to nil. Mars was a big planet. The colonies, specks in all that vastness. And since most colonists never left the domes, that cut the chances even more.

Plus there was the fact the Martians didn't show up on their sensors. If not for motion trackers, the Martians *would* be invisible.

Archard tried to work out how that could be. Mars was a cold planet. Far colder, on average, than Earth. It stood to reason that any life that evolved must either generate enough heat to survive or be cold-blooded, like reptiles, fish and crustaceans on Earth. So cold-blooded, in fact, they didn't have heat signatures.

Now that Archard thought about it, those things in the cavern, with their carapace-protected bodies—biologists called those exoskeletons—and their jointed legs, might well be crustaceans. A far more intelligent breed than their cousins on Earth.

Archard was brought out of his musing by a sharp pain in his side. He had run so far, he was hurting. He could hear Everett pant. McNee, iron-hard with muscle, barely breathed heavy.

"Stop," Archard said. "We'll rest a minute." He checked his motion sensor.

"Can you tell us what you saw, sir?" Sergeant McNee said.

"A whole city," Archard said, and only now did it fully sink in.

"Those we killed must be their soldiers," Sergeant McNee said.

"We don't know that."

"A lot of species have soldiers, sir. Army ants. Beetles. Other bugs. Why not Martians? The way they came after us. Aggressive. Hostile."

Archard was about to say that he didn't believe the Martians were insects when his helmet blared.

"Captain! Captain! Can you hear me? This is Pasco."

Archard didn't like the panic in his voice. "I can hear you. Report, Private."

"We need help! Hurry! We're under attack!"

16

They had been running for so long, Archard was soaked in sweat. Every sinew ached. Only sheer will kept him going.

The locator beacons proved their worth. If not for their signals, Archard could easily see he and the others becoming hopeless lost. The many forks, the many branches, were a maze.

He kept trying to raise Private Pasco without success. Pasco had gone quiet after the initial contact, and Archard feared the worst. If the Martians could burrow through basalt, and through the walls of a module, it was conceivable they might be able to bore through the otherwise impregnable armor on the tank.

"I don't know how much longer I can go on," Private Everett huffed. He had fallen slightly behind and was struggling to keep up.

"There are no quitters in the U.N.I.C.," Sergeant McNee said. "You'll do as we damn well tell you."

The Kentuckian weaved and stumbled.

Archard tried his helmet comm again. "Private Pasco, can you read me?" All he heard was the muted hiss of the circuit. "Pasco? Do you read? What's happening up there? Status report."

"It could just be interference," Sergeant McNee said. "Reception can be spotty underground."

Archard was well aware of typical communications issues but it didn't ease his worry any. Not just for Pasco and the boy. Losing them would be tragic. Losing the tank would be a death sentence. He and the others didn't have enough air to make it back to New Meridian on foot. Trying not to dwell on that, he said, "Pasco, damn it!"

His helmet crackled. "Sir? Sir? Is that you? Where have you been? I've been trying to raise you."

"Report," Archard commanded.

"We're still here. I guess it wasn't an attack, after all. I don't know what it was. Or is, since they're still out there."

"Pasco, I need you to make sense. What are they doing?"

"Nothing. Well, that's not true. They're just standing there. Must be forty, fifty maybe. They have us surrounded and they're staring at us with the weirdest eyes you can imagine. Studying us, I think. What do I do?"

Archard remembered the creature that studied him, and how Piotr had said the things studied the remains of his parents. Were the Martians trying to make sense of what they were seeing? After all, humans must be as alien to them as they were to humans. "Sit tight. Don't do anything. We'll be there in five. How's your charge?"

"My what? Oh. The kid. He's still asleep."

"With the Martians all around?"

"I didn't think it right to wake him. The poor little guy has been through a lot."

"Hang steady. See you soon."

They were approximately fifty meters from the cave entrance when Archard spied a hole in the side of the tube. He was sure it hadn't been there when they descended. Evidently, the creatures surrounding the tank had come out of it.

He hand-signaled to the others to slow to a walk, then stalked forward as quietly as possible. When the tank came into view, he froze.

It was exactly as Paso described. Dozens of creatures, their stalk eyes moving back and forth and up and down, as if they were mesmerized. Or taking in every little detail.

"Pasco?" Archard whispered.

"Sir?" the Spaniard replied much too loudly.

"We're about to make a break for the tank. Be ready." Archard turned to the others. "Locked and loaded?"

"Let's do this," Sergeant McNee said.

17

"Pick your targets," Archard gave a last command. "We don't want to damage the tank by mistake and be stranded."

"I hear that," Private Everett said.

Archard moved into the open and the nearest Martian turned and raised its eye stalks. Not a second later, all the rest did the same.

Archard's skin crawled. He took a slow step and was immediately flanked by Sergeant McNee and Private Everett.

The creatures exploded toward them.

Archard sprayed Martian after Martian. To either side, Sergeant McNee and Private Everett poured their own auto-fire into the surging tide. It dropped the foremost ranks but didn't deter the rest.

Archard dropped a creature with its legs spread wide, shifted, and drilled another. He thought he heard Private Pasco shout something in his comm-link but he couldn't be sure.

A Martian reached Everett. A leg speared into his EVA suit, thigh-high, before Everett cut the thing down. The hole was small enough that the suit instantly sealed the breach.

Archard shot and shot and shot again, narrowly avoiding having his own suit ripped. The press of Martians forced him back a couple of steps. Private Everett prudently retreated, too.

Sergeant McNee didn't notice. The non-com stood his ground, meeting the Martian wave with sweep after sweep of his ICW.

Private Pasco sprang out of the tank airlock and joined the fray, sending lead into the creatures from their rear.

McNee looked up, taking his eyes off the Martians for only a moment. Executing a high bound, one of the things slammed into his chest. McNee clubbed it with his stock as its grippers sheared into his suit. His head snapped back and his mouth widened from the pain.

Archard shot once, twice, three times, and it sagged and fell from the non-com's chest.

McNee dropped to his knees.

Archard darted over as Private Pasco gave out a whoop. The few remaining Martians were bee-lining into the lava tube. The dead lay in heaps, with wounded ones here and there waving their eyes and legs, but none could stand.

"Sergeant? Can you hear me?"

There was a large hole in the front of McNee's EVA suit, much too large for the suit to repair. His face was nearly blue.

Quickly, Archard wrapped an arm around him. "Help me!" he bawled at Everett and Pasco. They bore McNee to the tank and Archard went through the airlock holding him.

Once inside, Archard eased the non-com onto his back in the bay. McNee was gulping for breath, his eyes so bloodshot, they appeared red. From the hole in his suit came sucking sounds. The Martian leg had speared through into his lung.

"Don't you die on me, Sergeant," Archard said. "I need you, damn it."

"Sorry, sir," Sergeant McNee said, blood dribbling from his mouth. He arched his back, gasped, "On Mars?" and was gone.

"This is bad," Private Pasco said.

"We haven't seen anything yet," Private Everett predicted.

Archard agreed. He had a foreboding feeling that things would soon become a lot worse.

OUTBREAK

18

Chief Administrator Levlin Winslow was having a terrible day. There hadn't been any word from Captain Rahn after his initial profoundly disturbing call. Winslow had the Communications Center try to raise the captain repeatedly, but there was no reply.

Winslow had an important call of his own to make, and he couldn't do it at the office. Secrecy was essential. His superiors had drilled that into him during his indoctrination for the administrator position. He left early, and headed home.

As if the situation at the Zabinski farm wasn't calamity enough, Winslow had another problem to deal with. Some of New Meridian's surveillance cameras were malfunctioning. A short in the system, the Chief of the Maintenance Center assured him. They'd have it fixed by morning.

Then there was his wife. She called a couple of hours ago to ask if he would bring home a bottle of alcohol-free wine. Why she bothered with the stuff was beyond him. Something in her tone told him that she was upset but she didn't bring up why and he wasn't about to set her off by asking.

Now, having washed his hands as she always made him do before he could sit at the supper table, Winslow glumly regarded his reflection in the bathroom mirror. It was hell being the most important person in the colony. The stress of the job was getting to him. His receding hair was grayer than when he arrived on Mars, his pudgy body, pudgier.

Squaring the shoulders he didn't have, Winslow boldly marched to the dining room table.

Gladys was already there, her heavily made-up face set in stern lines, tapping her long red fingernails on her plate.

Cringing inside, Winslow forced a smile. "How do you do, my dear? May I say you looking ravishing tonight?" He was terrible at flattery, but if it blunted her wrath, he would try.

"Spare me," Gladys said. "You forgot again, didn't you?"

"I told you I would be a little late," Winslow said, thinking she was upset because she'd had to keep supper waiting.

"Not that, you simpleton."

"Honestly, dear, how can you talk to me that way? I'm your husband."

"Don't remind me. You're piss-poor at it so it's nothing to brag about." Gladys made a tent of her fingers and glared. "What day is it?"

"Oh hell," Winslow said without thinking. Frantic, he ran down the list. Her birthday was months away. It wasn't Valentine's Day or some other holiday.

"Think, Levlin," Gladys said, dripping venom. "What did you and I do twenty-eight years ago today?"

"Exchanged vows," Winslow remembered, and braced for the tirade to come.

His phone chirped. Eagerly grasping at salvation, Winslow snatched it from his pocket. "Hold on, dear. This might be important." Hopefully it was word that Communications had heard from Captain Rahn. "Chief Administrator here."

"Sir, it's Ferguson."

"You have good news, I trust?" Winslow said to his assistant.

"We have a problem."

"Can't you deal with it?" Winslow demanded.

"No, sir. Your presence is required at the Maintenance Center."

Winslow didn't contain his annoyance. "Is this about those cameras shorting out? I told them to deal with it. What can possibly demand my personal attention?"

Ferguson lowered his voice, or else was holding his hand partly over the receiver. "Two of the maintenance workers have disappeared."

"What do you mean, disappeared? We're in a dome. There's nowhere for them to go. They probably snuck off to the Social Center for a drink."

"No, they didn't."

"How can you be so sure?" Winslow angrily demanded.

"Because, sir," Ferguson said, whispering now, "there's an awful lot of blood."

19

Winslow never liked visiting the Maintenance Center. For one thing, the place smelled of lubricants and solvents and the like. He could do without that, thank you very much; he positively dreaded getting the stuff on his suits. He was Chief Administrator, for God's sake, not a grease jockey, as they used to be called.

The M.C. was responsible for fixing everything that broke, from rovers to computers. On Earth, the work was more specialized. There were vehicle repair shops and electronic shops, etc. On Mars, the powers-that-be believed it wiser to combine specialties. That way, fewer colonists were required to do comparable tasks. A critical aspect, given that space in the domes was limited.

The domes themselves were masterpieces of Earth technology. Constructed of an indestructible alloy covered by a protective nanosheath, they were breathtaking to behold. From the outside, in sunlight, they gleamed like gold.

Bradbury, the first colony, had three domes. Wellsville, the second, had added a second dome about a decade ago. New Meridian only had one dome, but Winslow was confident that under his leadership, New Meridian would qualify for a second and even a third dome in record time.

He'd never said anything to anyone, but he thought it silly to have named the first two colonies after long-dead-and-buried writers. Personally, he found reading a chore. Why read a book when you could have your computer or your eReader read it to you? At his office, he never read a document longer than two pages. He had Ferguson read them and provide a summary.

As his chauffeur brought the official vehicle to a stop, Winslow smoothed his suit, ran a hand over his thinning hair, and waited impatiently for the woman to open his door. "About time."

Overhead, the high vault of the dome presented the illusion of blending into the sky. The alloy and the nanosheath were transparent, so that from inside it was if nothing were there.

Psychologists claimed it made Mars seem more like 'home,' and the domes less like the environmental cages they were.

Those same psychologists, and behavioral scientists, also had a large hand in the layout of the buildings and streets. Everything was Earth-like, specifically so the colonists would feel more comfortable.

Ever since an early expedition in which half a dozen astronauts lived on Mars for a year to see how it affected the human organism, and one of them cracked up and killed two others, the 'comfort zone,' as the big brains called it, was considered crucial.

With a sigh, Winslow turned to the Maintenance Center. In his opinion, it was the ugliest building in New Meridian. Slate grey, and fashioned to look metallic, it brought to mind one of those old-time garages. A blight, if you asked him, on the colony's beauty.

The front door hissed and out hustled Ferguson. A reed of a man, he wore a pink suit that matched his spiked pink hair. He also wore a pink nose ring, which irritated Winslow no end. A nose should be a nose, not a decoration, especially on a government official.

"Thank goodness you're here, sir. I don't know how much more of this I can take. I don't know what to think. I truly don't."

Winslow held up a hand to stem the deluge. "Compose yourself, man. Take deep breaths. It can't be as bad as all that."

"You haven't seen, sir," Ferguson said, and shuddered.

Another figured ambled out, a woman in a brown maintenance uniform, her hair cut short, her eyes hazel. She was wiping her hands on a dirty rag. Rachel Adams was her name, and she was Head of Maintenance. "Chief Administrator Winslow. How's it hanging?"

"*Must* you always be so crude?" Winslow responded.

"Bugs you, does it?" Rachel said. "Well, brace yourself for worse. I think we have a murder on our hands."

20

On the ground floor of the Maintenance Center, to one side of the vehicle repair bay, was a sizeable office filled with monitoring stations. Dozens of small screens linked to cameras throughout New Meridian lined the walls. Some showed street scenes. Others, the dome, from various points. Still others had been set up in maintenance tunnels and conduits.

Rachel Adams led Winslow to a central work station and motioned for the person manning it to move aside. Sinking into the chair, Rachel flicked a switch and a screen that showed a street scene went black. "There you go."

Winslow didn't understand. "It's too late in the day, and I'm too tired for games. Why am I looking at a blank screen?"

"You're not supposed to be. The camera for section three of sublevel corridor B stopped working earlier today," Rachel explained. "We didn't think much of it at the time. Now and then that happens. A breaker trips, a component overheats, what have you. We scheduled an inspection for tomorrow. It hardly seemed urgent."

"Yes, so?"

"So a couple of hours later, a camera for another section of sublevel corridor B went dark, too. That was a bit strange. But what really got my attention was when a third camera went out. That's when I called your office. I was concerned there might be some sort of system-wide problem developing. "

"Back up." Winslow was picturing the sublevels in his mind's eye. He'd only been down there once, on his initial tour of the dome. All he could recall was a bewildering network of passageways, pipes, conduits, and junction boxes. The literal underbelly of New Meridian. "Was the third camera on sublevel corridor B, as well?

"It was, in fact," Rachel confirmed. "I sent Fortier and Zuka down. My best electricians. They reported hearing sounds—"

"Sounds?" Winslow interrupted. "What kind of sounds?"

"They weren't sure."

"This gets stranger and stranger," Winslow said.

"Doesn't it, though."

"Go on."

"Well, we had them in sight until they entered the stretch where the last camera went out. Zuka radioed in that they could see the camera, that it had fallen from its mounting and was lying in pieces. Which didn't make sense. The mounts are metal brackets, and the cameras are bolted in place."

"And then?"

Rachel swiveled toward him and scowled. "Total silence. We waited for them to report in, but nothing. I tried to contact them. Still nothing. So I sent a tunnel rat down."

Winslow knew about those. Tunnel rats were miniature rovers used to ferry tools and whatnot, and for tunnel inspections.

"It's still down there. This is what its camera shows." Rachel tapped a button and the dark screen lit with the night-vision image of a broken camera and part of a casing about a meter away. It also showed a wide smear.

"Is that...?" Winslow said.

"The blood I told you about, sir," Ferguson said, swallowing.

The smear formed a trail that went around a corner. Lying here and there were small objects Winslow' couldn't quite make out. "What are those?"

"I'll give you a close-up," Rachel said. She tweaked a dial and the tunnel rat zoomed in.

For all of half a minute, Winslow was at a loss. Some of the objects were pulpy and pink. The largest was dark red. A pale stub, finger-length, caught his eye. He bent toward the screen, and gasped. It *was* a finger, severed off. "Is that...?"

"Lots of little body bits," Rachel said. "Murder. It has to be. Someone has gone off the deep end and is hiding down there. We have to find them before they kill anyone else." She smirked at Winslow. "And since Ferguson tells me that Captain Rahn and his boys left the dome early today, and you're our Chief Administrator, you'll have to lead the search team, yourself."

21

Winslow hated to be put on the spot, hated it more than anything. But the Head of Maintenance was right. As C. A., it *was* his job to oversee any crisis that cropped up. Normally, he would assign this to the security unit, but with the troopers gone, circumstances had boxed him in a corner. "Damn them anyhow," he muttered.

"Sir?" Ferguson said. "I didn't catch that."

Rachel spared Winslow from having to respond by saying, "Why did Rahn take his people out, if you don't mind my asking?"

"A missing child," was all Winslow was willing to reveal. It wouldn't be wise to let the cat out of the bag about the creatures Rahn claimed to have seen, especially since he hadn't had a chance to place his call to the governor yet. "I've tried to raise him on the radio but can't. Not that we need him to deal with a lone lunatic."

"You hope," Rachel said.

"I want everyone in maintenance, including those brawny fellows I saw working on a rover, to report to the sublevel access hatch in ten minutes."

Rachel sat back and folded her arms. "Hold on there, Chief. Everyone? That'll disrupt my whole schedule. Set me back hours."

"As you pointed out," Winslow said reminded her, "the evidence suggests a murder has been committed. I should say that catching the culprit is vastly more important." He indulged in a smirk. "What is your labor compliment at the moment, by the way?

"Nine in the building," Rachel said. "Four more are out on jobs."

"Nine is plenty," Winslow said confidently. "Have them bring tools and whatnot to defend themselves, should the need arise."

"Rope, too, sir," Ferguson said. "Or something else to restrain the individual responsible."

"Excellent suggestion," Winslow said, and his assistant beamed with pride. "Hop to it, Ms. Adams." And he beamed, too. Of his many duties, giving orders was the aspect he liked best. Telling people what to do gave him such a sense of power. It was even better that they had no choice but to do it.

Rachel switched on the Maintenance Center's public address system and told everyone to do as Winslow had instructed her.

The access hatch was the only way into the sublevels from maintenance. Other hatches were located in other buildings throughout New Meridian, but only maintenance personnel were allowed to use them.

Once her people had gathered, Rachel explained what they were about to do.

At an appropriate point, Winslow stepped forward. "Listen to me, all of you. As your administrator, my first priority is your safety. Exercise caution. Whether it was Mr. Zuka or Mr. Fortier who went off the deep end is irrelevant. We must place him in restraints so he can't harm anyone else. Working together, that shouldn't pose a problem. Not with as many of us as there are. Understood?"

All of them nodded or responded in the affirmative.

"Good." Winslow indicated the hatch. "Then down we go."

22

Winslow had forgotten how uneasy the sublevels made him. The tunnels were narrow, and cold. The air was thinner because there were fewer ventilation shafts, and the lighting left a lot to be desired, too. He imagined the murderer lurking in every shadow, waiting for a chance to strike.

Like a commander in the military, Winslow barked orders. He had the five biggest workers go ahead of everyone else. The rest brought up the rear. Which left him safely in the middle.

"Go slow," Rachel cautioned her people. "We don't know what we're dealing with here."

"A lunatic, obviously," Ferguson said. "He's gone Mars Happy."

Winslow was inclined to agree. "Mars Happy" was a less than technical term for those rare instances in which a colonist snapped. Despite the extensive screening of Mars applicants, it had happened twice. In the first instance, at Bradbury, a male nurse left a note saying that he missed Earth so much, he couldn't take it anymore, and slit his wrists. The second time, at Wellsville, a chemist left a video in which he said he was going to 'become one' with Mars. Then he walked out a dome airlock—without an EVA suit.

Winslow grimaced in revulsion. He never could get used to the crazy things people did. "What about Zuka and Fortier? Did they dislike one another?"

"Quite the opposite," Rachel said. "They were the best of friends."

"Yet one of them killed the other," Ferguson said.

"Or someone else snuck down here and murdered both," Rachel said.

Winslow almost broke stride. He hadn't considered that possibility. He put it from his mind and paid attention to the tunnels. Not that he had the slightest idea where they were in relation to the hatch. The many turns they'd made were too confusing.

Suddenly, the men in front stopped, bringing everyone to a standstill.

"What's the holdup?" Rachel hollered.

"The lights up ahead are out," the lead man said. "The tunnel is completely dark."

By rising onto his toes, Winslow confirmed that they were. "Doesn't anyone have a flashlight?" He certainly didn't go around with one in his pocket. To his consternation, none of the maintenance workers did, either.

"We'll have to send someone back," Rachel said.

The big man in the lead called out, "Do you hear that, Chief Administrator?"

In the silence that fell, Winslow swore he could hear his own breathing. He also heard, from out of the darkness, peculiar noises. Tapping, it sounded like. And scraping.

"What on earth?" Rachel Adams said, and raised her voice. "Fortier? Zuka? Is that you up there? Come out where we can see you."

Ferguson put a hand to his throat and took a step back. "Please don't let there be violence. I can't stand violence. It's ugly. It makes me physically ill."

The big man in the lead yelled to Rachel, "Misha and Renaldo and me will go find out who it is, if you want us to."

"Are you sure, Sam?" Rachel said.

"I have this," Sam said, and hefted a wrench as long as his arm.

"Be careful."

Sam nodded, and he and the others edged forward. One by one the darkness swallowed them.

Winslow admired their courage. He wouldn't do that for anything.

"Sam's a good man," Rachel said. "He can bench press four hundred. If anyone can handle…" She stopped short.

A sharp cry came out of the darkness. Then another. And the sounds of a scuffle.

"Sam?" Rachel cried. "What's going on?"

Something exploded out of the dark. Winslow had a fleeting impression of long legs and an impossible shape, and then the thing was on the first man in line. The man screamed as an alien limb was thrust clear through his chest and out his back.

Winslow felt his bladder go. He went, too, turning and shoving past Ferguson, who was riveted in shock. Shouldering a shocked Rachel Adams aside, Winslow barreled through the rest. More screams rose, and he glanced back to see that the hideous monstrosity wasn't alone. Half a dozen of the things were slaughtering the Maintenance people, literally ripping them apart. Rachel Adams was down, fighting for her life. Poor Ferguson had backed against a wall, blubbering hysterically. He just stood there as a creature seized him by the head, and tore his head off.

Winslow fled pell-mell. He was crying, and blinked away tears. Not for the others. For himself. He didn't want to die. "Please, please, please, no, no, no, no!" he sobbed, and ran as he had never run before.

Only now did he remember Rahn saying that the security unit had gone after some kind of 'creatures.' These must be the same things, he realized. He hadn't thought it remotely possible they could get into New Meridian, not with the dome.

Winslow took turn after turn, not knowing where he was going. He was running to put distance between himself and the abominations that attacked the others. His heart pounded. He sweated buckets. His legs became welters of pain.

God or Fate or sheer dumb luck were kind to him. Winslow rounded a turn and there was the open hatch. He went up the ladder two rungs at a time. Gasping and sobbing, he slammed the hatch shut and worked the wheel to secure it.

Tottering back, Winslow wiped his brow, and laughed. He'd done it! He'd escaped! But now what? Should he spread an alarm? Or wait for Captain Rahn to return and have the soldiers take over.

Steadying his wobbly legs, Winslow hurried away. He couldn't stand the wet feeling of his pants, and the smell. He needed to shower and change. He had plenty of time. The things were contained in the sublevel; they couldn't get through the hatch. The colony was safe for the time being.

Before he showered, though, he had that special call to make to the governor.

RED PLANET RISING

23

No one spoke on the ride back to New Meridian. Even Private Pasco, for once, shut up.

Archard left the driving to Everett while he tried to raise the colony. A systems check showed that their communications equipment was in working order. The calls should go through, yet didn't.

An atmospheric fluke of some kind, Archard figured. He decided to raise Wellsville and have Captain Howard get in touch with Chief Administrator Winslow. But Wellsville didn't respond, either.

Troubled by the seeming coincidence, Archard attempted to get through to Bradbury. After a dozen tries, he sat back in his seat and broke the long silence with, "Son of a bitch."

"Sir?" Everett said.

Archard didn't see any reason to keep it from them. "I can't get through to any of the colonies."

"All three?" Everett said in disbelief. "How is that possible?"

From the bay, Pasco said, "A sandstorm would have to cover half of Mars for that to happen. Do the weather updates mention one?"

Private Everett gestured at the windshield. "Do you see a storm?"

"No sandstorms," Archard said to forestall an argument. "And everything is in working order."

"Something's not right, sir," Everett said.

Archard agreed. "But what?" he wondered aloud.

"If you don't know, sir, I sure don't," Pasco said. "You're a lot smarter than me."

Archard consulted the holo map. "We're less than ten minutes out of New Meridian. We'll put through calls to the other colonies when we get there." He twisted in his seat to check on Piotr.

The Zabinski boy had woken up shortly after the firefight, and ever since had sat huddled in a corner. He continued to clutch his mother's head as if it were a security blanket.

Archard had been gentle before because of the circumstances, but it couldn't go on. Rising, he walked back and squatted. "Piotr?"

The boy stared off into space. He didn't blink, didn't twitch a muscle.

"Piotr?" Archard was afraid he'd gone into shock, a delayed reaction to the living nightmare he'd endured.

"Piotr, can you hear me?"

The boy's chin dipped.

"Good," Archard said. "We're almost to New Meridian. You'll be fed and cleaned up and taken care of. You have friends there, don't you? People your parents knew? Other kids you visited?"

Piotr's throat bobbed.

"I'm sorry for your loss," Archard said. "I truly am. But you can't go on holding you mother's head." He held out his hand. "Give it to me, if you would."

"No."

"Please. I will see that nothing happens to it. I promise."

Piotr blinked, and tears formed at the corners of his eyes. "It's my mom."

"It's just her head."

The boy hugged it tighter. "It's all I have. Those things wanted her but I wouldn't let them take her."

"Look at her, Piotr."

Piotr shook his head.

"Look at what you are holding."

"I don't want to."

"You *have* to," Archard insisted. If the boy didn't, he would take it by force.

Piotr looked down.

In life, Ania Zabinski had been pretty. In death, her face was hideous. Her glazed eyes had rolled up, showing the whites. Dry blood caked her chin and dotted her sunken cheeks. Her mouth was set wide, her teeth bared. As if that weren't enough, the strips of flesh that dangled from her neck had gone stiff and were discolored.

Uttering a low whine, Piotr dropped the head as if it were about to bite him. He covered his faceplate with his arms and burst into tears.

"I'm sorry." Archard put a hand on the boy's shoulder but Piotr shrugged it off. "All right. We'll leave you alone." Picking up the head, he stepped to a storage locker and placed it inside.

"Poor kid," Pasco said.

"Stay by him," Archard directed.

"Like his shadow," Pasco said.

Archard returned to his seat. The dome was in sight, glistening golden in the pale Martian sunlight.

"Another couple of minutes and we'll find out what's going on," Private Everett said.

Archard couldn't wait.

24

Chief Administrator Levlin Winslow was confused. He'd tried and tried to contact Governor Blanchard on their private line but the governor didn't answer.

Thinking a storm must be to blame, Winslow got on the horn to New Meridian's satellite people and they informed him the skies over both colonies, and in-between, were clear.

Winslow clicked off and sat at his desk glaring at his screen. If it wasn't the weather, then it must be an equipment glitch. Normally, he would ring maintenance and have them fix things. But most of the maintenance staff were in bits and pieces down in sublevel two.

Winslow needed to keep a clear head and think things through. It was important that word be relayed to Earth, that they be made aware it had finally happened.

Winslow was so engrossed in mulling his options that when his computer chirped, he jumped. He accepted the call and felt a wave of anger at the image that resolved. "Captain Rahn! Where the hell have you been? You should have been back hours ago. I've been trying to reach you—"

"And I've been trying to reach *you*," Rahn cut him off. "We're fifty meters from the main airlock. I was finally able to get through."

"I trust you have a good explanation for why I couldn't raise you," Winslow indignantly began, but once again the captain rudely interrupted.

"We followed the things that killed the Zabinskis from their farm to Albor Tholus. As incredible as this will sound, there's an entire underground city. These aren't just animals. They're *Martians*. Intelligent, like us. With their own civilization, like us. We were forced to engage, and lost Sergeant McNee."

"You've *seen* a Martian city?" Winslow said. The cat was out of the bag in more ways than one. He wondered how the bigwigs back on Earth would take the news. Fully half a minute went by before he realized Rahn had gone quiet. "Captain?"

"What the hell?" Rahn said.

"I beg your pardon?"

"You know about them."

"What?" Winslow said, his voice rising. "No. Of course not. Not before today."

"You're lying."

"How dare you?" Winslow said. "You're talking to your superior." Anxious to divert the officer's suspicion, he quickly went on. "And for your information, those farmers aren't the only ones the Martians attacked. Rachel Adams and most of her maintenance crew were slaughtered a while ago."

"Why didn't you tell me that straight away?"

"Damn it, Captain. I'm extremely rattled here. We've got real, live Martians, and dead colonists, and I haven't been able to get through to Bradbury or Wellsville."

Archard seemed to bend into the screen. "You're telling me that New Meridian's communications are down except for intercolony?"

"Evidently," Winslow nodded. "And no one knows why."

"If the weather isn't a factor, and our equipment is working, that leaves..." Rahn blinked a few times.

"Yes?" Winslow said.

"It sounds as if we're being jammed."

"Jammed?" Winslow repeated as a horrifying possibility occurred to him, an idea so terrible, an invisible fist closed on his chest.

"We're being denied satellite access," Rahn was saying. "I can't think of anything else that would account for it. But who would jam us? And why?" He sat straighter. "We're at the lock. Meet me at the Maintenance Center."

The screen went dark.

Winslow didn't move. He quaked and said under his breath, "God, no. God, no. God, no. God..."

25

At first glance, New Meridian appeared normal. Businesses were open. People moved about as they usually did. A mother and her little girl smiled and waved at the tank. A man poked his thumb at the dome as if to say 'Keep up the good work.'

Archard directed Private Everett to make straight for the Maintenance Center. He had a sinking feeling in his gut that a disaster was in the making unless he dealt with the Martians quickly.

Craning his neck, Archard regarded the scientific marvel that protected them from the elements and enabled them to exist on a hostile planet. Nothing could penetrate that dome. Or so the experts claimed. But no one had given any thought to a colony being invaded from *below*.

Private Pasco piped up from the bay seat, "Sir, shouldn't we strip out of our EVA suits?"

"Not yet," Archard said. "We might need them."

"*Inside* the dome?" Pasco said incredulously.

"You heard me." Archard was concerned about an atmosphere breach. Granted, the creatures had undoubtedly burrowed into New Meridian, and not gotten through the dome itself. But he must keep every contingency in mind.

"We're here," Private Everett said, and braked. "What about McNee? And the boy?"

"Leave the body for now," Archard said. "Pasco, bring Piotr."

The front door wasn't locked. Except for the hum of machinery, the whole place was quiet. No workers were anywhere to be seen.

Archard proceeded to the office. He noticed right away that an unusual number of monitor screens were black. Most of the sublevel cameras, it turned out, were out of commission. The exceptions filled him with unease.

There were five access hatches to the sublevels, located throughout the colony. Surveillance cameras, and lights, were positioned near each. And those five cameras were the only sublevel cameras still working. They showed the adjoining tunnels were all dark. Every sublevel section, *except directly under the hatches.*

The Martians had deliberately left the access ladders well lit.

Why? Archard asked himself. So the Martians could see anyone coming down? Unlikely, since the creatures had shown they were perfectly capable of getting around in near-complete darkness.

Archard could think of only one other explanation. The lights were on under the hatches to lull humans into a false sense of security. Which implied the Martians were using psychological warfare tactics. And *that* implied a lot more.

Shaking his head, Archard said to himself, "What the hell are we up against?"

"Looks like everything is secure, sir," Private Everett said. "The hatches are still sealed."

Archard didn't point out that the Martians didn't need the hatches; they could dig up through the foundation. He buzzed the hospital, asked for Dr. Dkany, and requested that she come over. "I'll explain when you get here."

Next, Archard tried to contact Chief Administrator Winslow but he didn't answer. "Damn him, anyhow."

"Sir," Private Pasco said. "Mind if I ask what the plan is?"

"In a very short while," Archard enlightened him, "we're going down into the sublevels and kill every Martian we find."

"Outstanding," Private Everett said.

26

Few people ever impressed Archard as much as Dr. Katla Dkany. Physician, surgeon, scientist, she always wore a white lab coat while on duty. Her long blonde hair, habitually in a ponytail, and her lake-blue eyes, appealed to his Germanic nature.

But it was her dedication to her job, and especially how efficiently she carried it out, that appealed to him more.

Archard liked order and discipline. He was a soldier, after all. He liked things to run smoothly. He liked people who ran smoothly, too, as it were. And no one he'd ever met was more on top of their game than Katla Dkany.

When she swept into the Maintenance Center, stepping quickly as was her wont, Archard couldn't help but smile. A tingle of pleasure rippled through him as he recalled their recent night together. "Dr. Dkany. Thank you for getting here so quickly."

Her eyes twinkling, Katla leaned in close to whisper, "Your teeth are showing. Be careful or your men will suspect."

Both Everett and Pasco were staring at him quizzically.

With a cough, Archard introduced them, then motioned for the latter to step aside. Behind Pasco stood Piotr, slumped in misery.

"What in the world," Katla exclaimed. Squatting, she raised the boy's chin, and gasped. "What's happened to this child? Who is he? He appears to be in shock."

Briefly, sticking to the essentials, Archard related the attack on the farm, and the aftermath.

Katla's astonishment was evident. "Martians? The Zabinski's dead? Sergeant McNee, as well? Why hasn't an alert been sounded? The other colonists need to know."

"I was going to have Winslow do that," Archard said, "but he hasn't shown up."

"I'll go to the Broadcast Center and see to it personally," Katla said, rising with an arm around Piotr. "Right after I drop this poor child at the hospital."

"Good. Then my men and I can get to the sublevels."

"Finally," Private Everett said.

Katla hesitated. "Although by rights I should go with you."

"How do you figure?" Archard said, thinking she was worried for him.

"Have you forgotten?" Katla said. "My primary specialty is medicine. I also minored in exobiology."

"Too dangerous."

"I might be of help," Katla persisted. "My training, my insights."

"What about the alert? And the boy?" Archard took her by the elbow and Piotr by the shoulder and guided them out of the office. "Have everyone stay inside and keep their EVA suits handy."

"If it must be," Katla said reluctantly. She made as if to kiss him on the cheek but caught herself. "Be careful. All of you."

"Goes without saying," Archard said. He held the door and as soon as they stepped through, he unslung his ICW and returned to his men. "We're not waiting for the C.A. any longer. Lock and load."

At a jog, Archard led them to the access hatch. The privates covered him as he opened it. Lying flat, he poked his head down. Except for the patch of light directly below, the connecting tunnels were pitch black.

Swiveling on his belly, Archard lowered his legs, placed them on either side of the ladder, and slid down rather than climb. At the bottom, he crouched and splayed his spotlight right and left. Nothing showed on infrared, which was par for the course. He tweaked his audio gain as high as it would go, with the same result.

At his gesture, Everett and Pasco quickly joined him, and the latter said, "Do you think they're out there, watching us?"

Archard was about to reprimand him for breaking silence when distant rustling and scrabbling filled his earphones.

The Martians were there, all right, rushing to the attack.

27

"Back to back," Archard ordered. "Everett, cover right. Pasco, left. I'll support."

They obeyed, standing straight and tall, the epitome of professional soldiers. No fear showed on either.

The scrabbling noises were louder.

"Semi-auto, unless we're pressed," Archard said. "If we can't hold, we go back up the hatch."

"Wish I wasn't wearing this EVA suit," Pasco complained. "It slows me a little."

"Focus, trooper," Archard said.

And then there was no time for anything except trying to stay alive as Martians burst upon them from both sides in a coordinated attack.

Thunder filled the tunnels as Everett and Pasco opened up.

Archard triggered lead to the right, swiveled, and sent more into the pack coming from the left. He'd noticed that the humps in the middle of the carapaces seemed to be a weak spot. It took less ammo to bring them down when they were hit there. He shouted to let the others know but didn't know if they heard him.

The Martians streamed up and over their fallen, showing no regard for their wounded fellows. Or so Archard thought until he glimpsed a wounded creature being pulled away by others even as the main tide washed over it.

A creature leaped, and Archard riddled it before it could reach him.

He had the illusion he was staring into a sea of waving eyes and grippers. Three times he slapped in new magazines, and still they came, a seemingly endless ocean of alien forms.

Archard realized he and his men would run out of ammo before the Martians ran out of number. And if they were overwhelmed, the colony lost any hope it had of surviving.

Quick decisions. They were key to being a good officer. Even more importantly, they were the key to staying alive in the heat of combat. Archard made one now. He tapped the selector on his

ICW to switch to grenades and then tapped again to go from frag to incendiary. He fired a round down the tunnel on the right, spun, and fired another down the tunnel to the left. "Incendiaries!" he shouted. "Get down!"

All three of them dropped low.

Explosions lit the sublevel, and chemical fires converged on their position. Martians were fried in their shells, and the shelves consumed.

For several heart-searing moments, Archard thought he had miscalculated and the fire would reach him and his men but the flames stopped meters short.

Everett and Pasco drilled several charred, twitching creatures, and the tunnels became still.

It wouldn't stay that way for long. "Up the ladder," Archard barked. He saw that Pasco's leg was bleeding, and amended his order with, "Private Pasco, you first."

At the limit of his suit's range, Archard's display showed motion. A second wave was coming. "Move it!"

Pasco's leg nearly buckled. Everett had to help. They climbed much too slowly.

Archard's motion sensor was going crazy. He needed to delay the Martians. Switching from incendiaries to frags, he angled the ICW so the trajectory would be just right, and let fly to both sides. Throwing threw himself against the wall, he pressed flat just as the first grenade went off. The wall moved, or seemed to. The second blast almost blew out his eardrums; he should have lowered the volume on his helmet.

By then, Pasco was through the hatch and lending Everett a hand.

Archard flew up the ladder, his hands and feet barely touching the rungs. No sooner was he out than he ordered it shut and sealed.

They stood there, catching their breaths.

"This isn't good, is it, sir?" Pasco said.

The understatement of the century, Archard thought. "It's a disaster in the making."

28

Chief Administrator Levlin Winslow couldn't get the word out of his head. *Jammed*, Captain Rahn had said.

At first, the idea seemed preposterous. Why would Governor Blanchard authorize such a thing? The answer leaped out at him like a splash of cold water.

Now, on his way home instead of going to the Maintenance Center as Rahn wanted, Winslow kneaded his hands in his lap and told the chauffeur to go faster.

After the slaughter he'd witnessed in the sublevel, he wasn't about to go anywhere near maintenance.

Winslow would do whatever was necessary to survive. It didn't bother him in the least that he was turning his back on those he had been appointed to watch over. When it came to self-preservation, it was everyone for him-or-herself.

Night had fallen with its typical suddenness, and stars sparkled high above the dome. Winslow never could get used to how different Mars' sky was from the night sky on Earth.

They arrived at his house and the chauffeur came around to open the door, Winslow surprised her by saying as he climbed out, "Tamika, I won't need you the rest of the evening. Take it off and do as you please."

"Why, thank you, sir. That's kind of you."

The house was quiet. Winslow hoped that his wife was in bed. She relished her 'beauty sleep'—Lord knew, she needed it—and usually turned in early. He hastened to the living room, to the west wall, to a wide space between a chair and a silly painting his wife liked. He raised his thumb to the concealed scanner and spoke the confirmation code aloud. The recessed door hissed wide and he was about to descend when the sound of ice tinkling in a glass caused him to stiffen and turn.

Gladys was in her nightgown, her hooch halfway to her mouth. "What the hell, Levlin? You never told me that was there."

"Go back to bed, dear," Winslow tried.

Ignoring him, as she always did, Gladys came over. "I live here, the same as you. What is this?" She peered down. "Where does it lead?"

"Come with me and I'll show you," Winslow said to spare himself from having to provide a long explanation.

"Why didn't you ever tell me this was here? A secret stairwell, in my own house!"

At the bottom was a massive access door with a keypad. There was also a turn-wheel in case the electricity went out.

"Why, it's a vault of some kind," Gladys marveled.

"The proper term is Survival Shelter," Winslow set her straight. "In the old days, they were called panic rooms. It was where someone would go to be safe if their house was broken into." He smiled and patted the impregnable door. "The company had it installed. Only three people on Mars have one of these. Myself. Chief Administrator Reubens at Wellsville. And Governor Blanchard at Bradbury."

"How come only you three?"

"That should be obvious." Winslow puffed out his chest. "We're in charge. We're important. The company wants to keep us alive." He tapped the sequence of numbers to open the door.

Gladys snorted. "Don't flatter yourself. To them you're just another cog in their machine." She paused. "Hold on. Why are we down here?"

The door was slowly swinging open.

"As a precaution," Winslow said. He hadn't planned to have her join him but now he had no choice. "We're in peril of our lives."

With a loud click, the door came to rest. Inside was completely black. Winslow expected the lights to come on, and when they didn't, he groped about for a switch. Too late, he became aware of peculiar noises.

Out of the blackness poured Martians, the same as in the sublevel, their stalk eyes waving back and forth. Running past Winslow, they swarmed toward Gladys. She screamed and dropped her glass and turned to flee but the creatures brought her down before she could take a step.

Her terror-filled eyes locked on Winslow's in appeal but there was nothing he could do but stand frozen with fear as the things tore her limbs from her body.

Winslow felt his knees go weak as blood welled up out of Gladys' mouth and crimson sprayed from the stumps of her shoulders and thighs. Her torso flopped convulsively, then went limp.

Winslow fought down an impulse to heave.

A Martian gripped his wife's head and with astounding ease wrenched it off. Holding the head aloft, it scurried into the blackness.

Other creatures placed Gladys's arms and legs to either side of her body and moved back, their eyes bobbing up and down.

Winslow wished he would pass out. It would spare him the horror to come. But no such luck.

The next moment, the creatures turned toward him and closed in.

29

Dr. Katla Dkany couldn't blame Piotr Zabinski for being difficult, not after the ordeal the boy had been through. Twice he'd stopped and wouldn't go on. Each time, she dropped to a knee and spoke soothingly and coaxed him into continuing.

Piotr's eyes were empty pits, his face slack. She doubted he knew where he was or what they were doing.

When Piotr stopped a third time, Katla simply picked him up and carried him. It was imperative she make haste to the Broadcast Center and have them issue an alarm. But first she must drop Piotr at the hospital.

Katla couldn't get over Archard's revelation about there being real, live Martians. Ever since she was Piotr's age, back in Budapest, she'd cherished the dream that one day humankind would discover they weren't alone in the cosmos. Finding an advanced civilization might be too much to ask, but life of any kind would be a start.

Her dream was why she'd minored in exobiology, why she'd later volunteered for Mars. Not that she'd believed Mars harbored life. It was just that the Red Planet was one step closer to planets that might.

Katla walked faster. With the advent of night, lights had come on all over the colony. One of the brightest was the red cross on top of the hospital.

Not many people were out and about, which wasn't unusual. It was the supper hour for many.

Katla passed the ambulance, which seldom saw use, parked in its usual slot. The wide double-doors opened and she went to the front desk.

The Duty Nurse, Sharon, was on the phone, her other hand over her other ear as if to hear better.

"Speak slowly, sir. You're not making any sense." She saw Katla and held up a finger to indicate she would be with her in a bit. "You need to calm down, sir. Please. I can't help you if you're hysterical." She rolled her eyes as if to convey she was talking to a nutcase. "People don't just vanish, sir. Your wife has to be around there somewhere."

"What?" Katla said.

Intent on her call, Sharon turned away. "For the last time. Take deep breaths and compose yourself."

Katla didn't wait. She hurried down a hall, searching for the floor nurse.

Illness was rare on Mars. Colonists were chosen, in part, based on their genetics, and were as healthy as human beings could be. Accidents, though, still happened, and in the first room lay a man with his broken leg in a cast. In the second, a woman whose required regular checkup revealed that her blood pressure had risen to a troubling level, was hooked to a monitor.

"Have you seen the Floor Nurse? Nurse Johnson?" Katla asked.

Engrossed in an eReader, the woman looked up. "Dr. Dkany! I didn't hear you come in."

"Nurse Johnson?" Katla said.

"She was in to check on me about fifteen minutes ago." The woman chuckled. "Don't you love that accent of hers? They speak so cute Down Under, don't they?"

"Do you have any idea where she went?"

"She didn't say, sorry."

The other rooms in the wing weren't being used. Katla was about to return to the front desk when she saw that the emergency door at the far end of the hall was ajar.

Katla wondered if Nurse Johnson had stepped outside for some reason. Cradling Piotr, she hastened over and stuck her head out. "Johnson? Are you out here?"

In the dim shadows it was hard to see anything. Katla took a partial step and her foot bumped something. She looked down, and smothered an outcry. She had found Nurse Johnson.

Or what was left of her.

30

The sublevel screens in the Maintenance Center office were still dark except for those directly under the hatches. To Archard's consternation, the tunnel under the Maintenance Center hatch was as empty as the rest.

"They've taken all their dead away," Private Everett exclaimed.

"Do animals do that?" Pasco said. He was leaning on a desk to support his leg.

"These things have a civilization, like we do," Archard enlightened him. "They're not animals. They're intelligent."

"As smart as us, sir?" Pasco said.

"That remains to be seen." Archard scanned the rest of the screens. The street scenes appeared perfectly ordinary.

"Could it be the Martians who are jamming our communications?" Private Everett said.

Archard hadn't even considered that. He'd seen no evidence of advanced technology in the underground city. But then again, it might be so different from Earth tech, he wouldn't recognize it if it was right in front of him.

"This is turning into a regular war," Pasco said. "And there's just us three."

Archard turned. "Let me see that leg."

The wound wasn't bleeding much but it was deep enough to require stitches.

"One of those things tore through my suit as if it were paper," Pasco said.

"We showed them, though," Private Everett said. "Between here and back at that lava tube, we must have killed a hundred or more."

"Out of, what?" Archard said. "Tens of thousands? Millions?" He clasped an arm around Pasco's shoulders. "Let's get you to the tank."

"I can walk on my own, sir. I don't need to be babied."

"Zip your hole and limp fast."

"Yes, sir."

The air outside felt cool and fresh, even if it was pumped from the Atmosphere Center.

Archard breathed deep and stiffened.

"Was that a scream?" Everett said.

The cry was so faint, Archard couldn't be sure. He strained his suit to hear another but the night stayed quiet.

They used the tank's rear bay door instead of the airlock. Archard checked the sensors, and once again, they displayed nothing out of the ordinary.

Pasco was holding his leg and grimacing. "I feel hot. And a little woozy. You don't suppose those things can poison us, do you, sir? Like scorpions, say?"

Something else Archard hadn't considered, and probably should have. He needed to get his head together. "They don't have stingers."

Everett had started the tank and put it into gear. Just then the consoles speakers blared, and this time there could be no mistake.

A woman was screaming for dear life.

31

Dr. Katla Dkany had performed surgeries. She was used to blood, and to the sight of internal organs. But seeing Nurse Johnson's headless torso, with Johnson's arms and leg placed to either side and Johnson's stomach ripped open and her organs in a pile, caused Katla's gorge to rise. She tasted bile and swallowed it down.

Piotr Zabinski saw the remains, too, and came to explosive life. "Mom!" he screamed, struggling furiously to break free.

Katla held fast. "It's not your mother," she said, and slammed the door shut. The electronic lock activated, and a digital display read 'Secure.'

Katla didn't feel secure. The door had hung open for minutes. The creatures Archard had described might be in the hospital.

Breathless with worry, she backpedaled. Piotr still struggled, but weakly. His outburst had given way to bleak despair.

The blood-pressure patient had raised her head from her eBook. "Did I just hear a yell? Is everything all right?"

"There are things..." Katla began, and stopped. The woman would think she was crazy if she mentioned Martians. "You might want to keep your door closed." She did so before the woman could object.

The guy with the broken leg was watching a movie. He smiled and gave a little wave as Katla shut his door.

Sharon was hunched over her duty station, saying into her phone, "You heard your husband call out and you went into the living room, and there's blood all over but he's gone?"

"Hang up," Katla said.

Sharon motioned as if to say she couldn't.

"I mean it." Reaching down, Katla ended the call. "You need to pay attention."

"What on earth?" Sharon said. "That woman was beside himself. She was the third call tonight. She claimed..."

"I heard what she claimed," Katla cut her off. "Now you need to hear me. Lives are at stake." She paused.

"Lives?"

"There are creatures loose in New Meridian," Katla resumed, and held up her hand when the Duty Nurse went to speak. "Don't start asking questions! I don't have time to explain everything. Nurse Johnson is dead and we're in danger. I need you to make sure the stairwell door to downstairs is locked." The hospital basement served as their storage room, and their morgue.

"But...but..."

"Just do it," Katla said. "Be careful, and get back here as quick as you can."

Clearly bewildered, nodding and shaking her head, Sharon rose, came around, and ran down the opposite hall.

"Here," Katla said, and placed Piotr in the vacated chair. "Sit tight. I have things to do."

The first was to contact Archard. He answered right away. Keeping her voice as calm as she could, she told him about Nurse Johnson, ending with, "I haven't had a chance to go to the Broadcast Center yet. The alert hasn't been sounded."

"I'll see to it myself," Archard said. "Are you safe there for the time being?"

"We appear to be."

"Good. I have a scream to investigate. Then we'll proceed to the Broadcast Center. I should be at the hospital in twenty minutes, tops."

"No problem," Katla said with more confidence than she felt.

"Hang in there," Archard said, and hung up.

Katla leaned on the console and closed her eyes. "This can't be happening," she said, and yet it was. She must deal with it as she did any crisis. Rousing, she wondered what was keeping Sharon, and moved to the junction.

The stairwell door at the other end was wide open.

"Sharon? Where are you?" Katla called out.

Her answer came in the form of a harrowing shriek.

32

Private Everett turned into a side street and slowed at Archard's command.

Thanks to the behavioral scientists and their insistence that the colonies on Mars be as Earth-like as possible, New Meridian's dim streets mimicked those of Earth. A fact that, from a security standpoint, Archard never liked. But since crime was nonexistent, and until now, no one knew that the Red Planet harbored hostile life, where was the harm?

"Damn us for overconfident fools," Archard said.

"Sir?" Everett said.

"Nothing. Audio at max."

"Already is."

The street was deserted. Muffled voices came from a couple of house modules.

"There's nothing here, sir," Private Pasco said. "We should get to the hospital. My leg is starting to bother me real bad."

"Quiet." Archard thought he heard scratching. He bent toward the nearest speaker even though his helmet relayed everything the sensors picked up perfectly well. "Stop the vehicle."

Everett braked and looked around. "There's an alley on this side. Want me to hop out and investigate?"

"I'll do it."

"Can we take off our EVA suits yet?" Pasco requested. "The atmosphere is normal, isn't it?"

"Not yet," Archard said. If the dome were breached, catastrophe could occur in the blink of an eye. He went out the bay and was almost to the alley when a thought struck him. Stopping, he gazed upward.

The atmosphere. A human would die, horribly, if exposed to Mars', which was ninety-six percent carbon dioxide. Evidently the reverse wasn't true because the air in the sublevels was Earth air and it hadn't killed the Martians. How were they able to breathe when Earth air only contained about four percent carbon dioxide?

Then there was the air pressure. Under the dome, it was a hundred times greater than out in the open. How was it the Martians weren't crushed to a pulp? Were their thick shells a factor? Did the shells protect them like a diving suit protected a deep-sea diver at depths that would otherwise crush the human body?

So many questions. Archard cast them aside and entered the alley. He went its entire length but didn't find another victim. Returning to the tank, he settled back as Everett took the next left. They were midway along the block when the Kentuckian braked so sharply, Archard was almost thrown against the dash.

"What the hell?" Pasco blurted.

"There," Everett said, pointing. "Do you see, sir? It's a body."

All Archard could distinguish was a large lump lying at the corner of a building. He exited to investigate.

A woman, on her way home perhaps, had been jumped at the darkest spot on the street. It was the usual; her arms and legs had been torn off and placed by her torso. Her head, in keeping with the pattern, was missing.

But it wasn't her grisly remains that caused an icy fist to clamp on Archard's chest and cut off his breath. It was the depression in the ground near her. The same kind of depression he'd seen at the Zabinski farm.

The Martians were out of the tunnels and boring through the very ground.

Wheeling, Archard ran to the tank. "The Broadcast Center," he barked the moment he was in. "Step on it."

"What about my leg, sir?" Pasco said, his jaw clenched.

"It will have to wait," Archard said. So would Katla. Alerting the colony came first. Then they would hurry on to the hospital. He only hoped she stayed alive until he got there.

33

Levlin Winslow wailed like an infant when the Martians seized him. He expected to be torn to pieces, as they had just done to Gladys. He struggled, if feebly, and was on the verge of passing out when the most remarkable thing happened.

Four of the creatures lifted him bodily and bore him into the Survival Shelter. His wits swimming, he was dimly aware of being whisked through a gaping hole in the rear wall. The smell of dirt filled his nostrils. He realized they were traveling through a freshly-dug tunnel.

The Martians didn't need the sublevels to get around. They could go where they pleased, making their own passageways.

Winslow could barely see. They flew past a recess, and in it, something moved, something huge, something unlike the creatures carrying him.

Total blackness closed in.

Undeterred, the Martians swept him along with frightening rapidity. His weight was no hindrance; he might as well be a feather.

The nightmare took an eternity. Tunnel after tunnel, this way and that.

Winslow didn't resist. It wouldn't do any good. Besides which, he was thankful to be alive—and wanted to stay that way.

Presently, the dimmest of light alleviated the darkness. The source eluded him. The tunnels changed, too. They weren't dirt, they were rock.

They passed a junction, and down it he beheld another huge *something* moving away.

Winslow didn't try to make sense of it. He didn't try to make sense of any of this. How could he? He wasn't a scientist. He was a politician. His specialty was kissing the asses of those above him and telling those below him what to do.

He should have known not to trust his superiors. They'd lied to him, just as they'd lied to the colonists. To the entire population of Earth, for that matter.

With a suddenness that sent stark terror coursing through him, the creatures burst out of a tunnel onto a narrow walkway suspended high over God-knew-what. Above them stretched a vast space filled with walkways and arches and structures that defied description. Glancing down, Winslow beheld more of the same, going down, and down, into the bowels of Mars.

Pale light, filtering from above, lent a grey hue to the surreal scene.

Winslow closed his eyes to ward off dizziness. He never could tolerate heights. As a boy, on a dare, he climbed onto the roof of a neighbor's garage and become so scared, his father had to rescue him using a ladder.

The narrow walkway connected to a wider one, with creatures hurrying to and fro.

Despite himself, Winslow grew interested in the Martians. There were different kinds, large and small and in-between, in different colors, too. But all of them had certain physical traits in common, namely, multiple legs, and crab-like or lobsterish shells for bodies. Most also had those eerie eyes at the ends of waving stalks.

It was the latter that got to Winslow most. Especially when the eyes of every last Martian in sight swung toward him.

Yet another walkway brought them to a broad shelf and a towering edifice that appeared to have been carved out of the reddish-black rock. They scuttled through an arched entrance and ascended a ramp that brought them to a spacious chamber.

Martians were everywhere.

Winslow barely had time to take the spectacle in when the creatures bearing him came to a halt and let go. Unprepared, he fell hard, scuffing his elbows. He pushed to his knees and was going to rise but an iron vise clamped onto his neck from behind, holding him in place.

Bleating in fear, Winslow closed his eyes and braced for imminent death.

34

Dr. Katla Dkany was a healer. It was in her nature to help others. So when she heard the duty nurse scream, she reacted without thinking. She ran down the hall, calling Sharon's name.

About to plunge through the open stairwell door, Katla stopped. "Sharon? Are you there?"

From below, only silence.

"Sharon?" Katla gave the door a slight push, enough that she could cautiously peer in.

The light that usually lit the stairwell was gone, housing and all. It had been forcibly ripped out, taking a piece of the wall with it.

"Sharon?"

There wasn't any blood or body parts. Whatever had happened, Sharon might still be alive.

Katla swallowed, and swung the door open. She was peering down the stairwell when a hideous shape, using the rails as a ladder, scuttled onto the top rail and clung there.

For breathless instants neither of them moved, then a pair of stalks rose and inhuman eyes fixed on Katla.

"Dear God!"

The creature seemed as fascinated by her as she was by it.

Taking advantage, Katla sprang back and slammed the door. She pressed her shoulder to it, thinking the creature would try to batter it down. Over a minute elapsed, with her pressing so hard, her shoulder hurt, but nothing happened.

Katla sprinted to the front desk.

Piotr was where she had left him, his knees to his chest, his arms wrapped around his legs.

Scooping him up, Katla ran to the first patient's room and burst in.

The guy watching TV smiled sleepily. "Back again? Who's the kid?"

"You have to get up," Katla said. "We have to get out of here."

"Huh?" the man said.

"There are…" Katla refused to say "Martians." He would think she was crazy. "…things loose in the hospital. The soldiers will be here soon to pick us up."

"Hold on a minute," he said as she turned to go. "What are you on about? What kind of things? Where's Dr. Basiloff? He set my cast. I should talk to him."

"No time."

Katla raced to the next room. The blood pressure patient had curled onto her side and was asleep. Katla had to shake her twice to wake her.

"What? What's going on?" the woman mumbled in confusion.

"We must leave the hospital," Kata explained. "I'll disconnect you."

"I thought Nurse Johnson said I was to be hooked to the monitor until midnight? She was very specific. Where is she, anyhow?"

"Please," Katla said. "There's no time to waste." She sat Piotr on the bed and undid the wrist strap that read the woman's blood pressure, heart rate, and other signs.

A shadow filled the doorway. In hobbled the guy with the broken leg, on crutches, saying, "What the hell is going on? Tell me more about these 'things' you mentioned?"

"Things?" the woman said.

"Captain Rahn and his men ran into them out at the Zabinski farm," Katla said. "Now they're in New Meridian."

"Ran into what?" the man in the cast said.

Katla was spared having to explain by a loud crunching sound from the middle of the room.

Before their very eyes, the floor began to dissolve.

35

An array of transmission and receiver dishes, antennas, and other equipment, rose like a metal jungle from the roof of the Broadcast Center.

The heart of New Meridian's communications, the B.C. was responsible for relaying television and radio feeds from Earth, as well as airing original colony programming. It was also the hub of their Emergency Broadcast System.

Archard instructed Pasco to remain in the tank and took Private Everett with him. The day shift had gone off duty and the swing shift was working.

A receptionist typing on an ePad looked up from her work and blinked in surprise. "Captain Rahn, isn't it? What can we do for you?"

"I need to see the manager."

"I'm sorry. Mr. Studevant went home for the day. He'll be back in at eight tomorrow—"

"The assistant manager, then," Archard said curtly. "Or whoever is in charge."

"That would be Ms. Galice. But she's unavailable at the moment. She's in Studio B overseeing the nightly news. If you'll wait, I'll have someone take you there as soon as she's—"

Archard knew Ruth Galice. He'd dated her before he hooked up with Katla. "I know where it is," he said, sweeping past her desk.

The receptionist rose. "You can't go marching in on them. They're in the middle of a newscast."

"All the better."

The Broadcast Center's three studios were arranged as convex extensions of the central core. Studio B contained the news-and-weather set, mainly desks with large screens in the background.

Archard barged in. The newsman was reading copy about a possible fourth colony within the next decade. The camera people and other crew glanced around. So did the woman in charge.

Ruth Galice whipped off her headset and moved to block his way. "Archard?" she whispered. "What do you think you're doing?"

Archard strode past. A cameraman tried to stop him and he shoved the man aside. Now wasn't the time for niceties.

The anchor pair on the air sat slack-mouthed as he walked around between them and stared into the camera.

"Citizens of New Meridian. Pay attention. This is Captain Rahn, U.N.I.C. Under Article Three, Section B, Subsection N, paragraph four of the United Nations Colonization Protocols, as head of security for New Meridian, I formally declare a state of emergency and assume temporary command of the colony."

"What?" Ruth Galice said, coming forward. "Does Administrator Winslow know about this?"

"I repeat. This is a state of emergency. You are to get to your homes if you are not already there. Make sure your airlocks are secure. Under no circumstances should you venture outside until I give the all-clear."

"What *is* this?" Galice asked the question undoubtedly uppermost on every listener's mind.

"We are under attack," Archard addressed the camera, and when a crewwoman snorted in derision, he glared, then continued. "It sounds preposterous, I know. But indigenous lifeforms have already killed over a dozen people."

"Indigenous?" the newsman found his voice. "There's no such thing."

"Are you calling the captain a liar?" Private Everett said.

"But...but..." Ruth Galice got out.

The double doors burst inward. Martians streamed in, and were on the crew in a blur of long legs and waving eyes. A cameraman held out his hands to ward them off and lost both forearms when a Martian gripped them at the elbows, and wrenched.

Ruth Galice screamed and retreated but she wasn't fast enough. Her scream ended in a gurgle when a Martian tore her head from her shoulders.

"Sir!" Private Everett needlessly cried, and brought his ICW into play.

So did Archard. Flicking the selector to armor-piercing rounds, he stitched creature after creature. A wounded one teetered into a woman holding a clipboard and speared a foreleg through her chest.

Archard sprang to Everett's side so they were shoulder-to-shoulder. Their combined auto-fire riddled the things, felling many in their tracks.

Still more swarmed to the attack.

36

Chief Administrator Levlin Winslow hoped his bladder wouldn't let go. Again. He didn't want to die reeking of urine. He swallowed, or tried to, but his mouth was completely dry.

Winslow stayed perfectly still. The grip on his neck hadn't tightened but the threat was clear. He could see the ends of the segmented digits that were curled around his neck. They were sheathed in the same shell-like covering as the creatures that took him prisoner. Only they were bright blue.

A long limb, also blue, extended past his shoulder. The four alien fingers at the end of it gripped him by the front of his suit. As effortlessly as if he were a child's doll, he was raised off the ground and turned so he faced the thing holding him.

Winslow gasped. He was both terrified, and in awe.

The thing was ten times the size of those that invaded New Meridian. It had two eyes and eight legs, but its body, notably the forepart, was much bulkier. The torso, if that is what it was, tapered into the overlapping folds of a long tail. Every square centimeter was a vivid, beautiful blue.

"What *are* you?" Winslow blurted.

The thing raised him until they were face-to-eyes. And what eyes! As blue as the rest, multifaceted, sparkling like gems. Its stalks dipped and rose as it minutely examined Winslow from his hair to his shoes.

"I'm friendly," Winslow got out. He thought to hastily add, "And I'm an important person." Perhaps they would be less inclined to kill him if they were aware of his position. "I'm in charge of the colony."

Other Martians converged. Most were the small kind. A few were like this blue one, only not quite as big. In a far corner stood a singular creature with an oblong green body three meters high, unusually thick antenna and eye-stalks, and legs that splayed wider than the legs of the rest. It was the only one of its kind in the chamber.

An invisible stir rippled through the Martians. Every last one swung toward an opening in the rear wall.

Out of it came the strangest Martian yet. About a meter in length, it reared a good three meters high. Where most Martians had two sets of four-legs, this one had two sets of three. Midway up its craggy body were a pair of long "arms" with those remarkable digits. Its eyes were the largest of any Martian Winslow had seen, overshadowed by an obscenely huge, bowl-shaped carapace. And all of the creature, from top to bottom, was a bright yellow.

The newcomer came straight over. Others in its path moved aside, dipping their bodies as it passed.

It didn't take a genius to figure out that this new Martian was special, a leader, maybe.

Mustering a smile, Winslow croaked, "I'm a leader, too. We should sit down and discuss the situation."

The yellow Martian brought its eyes close to his. "Do you understand me? Is it possible for us to communicate?"

The yellow creature turned its eyes to the blue creature, and the blue creature slowly, almost casually, took hold of Winslow's left thumb and broke it.

Dr. Katla Dkany's could hardly credit her eyes. A hole was forming in the floor. The modules used in the buildings on Mars were supposed to be impenetrable but *something* was ripping through at a fantastic rate. Dust spewed, causing her to raise a hand to shield her face. She blinked and coughed and swiped at the dust, and when she could see again, she beheld what she took to be a giant drill. It was ridged like a drill, and tapered to a near-point. But then it stopped spinning and the ridges parted, and twin stalks emerged with eyes unlike any she ever conceived.

The blood-pressure patient screamed.

Instantly, the creature's eyes slid back into the ridges and the thing whisked down out of view.

"We have to get out of here!" Katla cried. Grabbing Piotr off the bed, she ran to the door but couldn't get through. The man with the crutches was rooted in astonishment. "Move! Hurry!"

"What *was* that?"

The woman in the bed screamed a second time.

A different creature was scrabbling out of the hole. One of the smaller, round Martians, the kind Katla had seen in the stairwell. It leaped to the end of the bed, raised its eyes and its bone-hard fingers, and was on the woman before she could move. A leg sheared into her bosom even as the creature gripped both sides of her head and tore it from her body.

The man on the crutches stumbled back, bleating in terror.

Another Martian was coming out of the hole.

Katla bolted from the room.

The man tottered and nearly fell. A crutch smacked the hall wall.

Katla wanted to help him but she knew if she did, she was dead. He couldn't move fast enough. Plus, she had Piotr to think of. She took a few more steps toward the hospital entrance.

"Wait!" the patient shouted. "Help me!"

Katla stopped. She couldn't do it. She couldn't desert another human being in need. She turned and reached out.

A Martian hurtled out of the doorway. It struck the man full in the chest, slamming him against the wall, and clung fast, its limbs churning. Flesh and blood sprayed high and low.

Katla ran. She made it as far as the front desk. The stairwell door down the other hall shattered and a Martian burst through. Darting behind the front desk, she crouched under it, holding Piotr tight.

"Lady," the boy said.

Startled that he had stirred to life, now of all times, Katla hushed him with, "Shhhh. Don't talk. We're in danger."

"Did you see the lady?"

"I did," Katla whispered. "But please. Not a word or they will do the same to us." She heard the clack of Martian limbs on the hard floor.

The noises stopped on the other side of the desk.

Katla dared not risk a peek. She could only pray the thing couldn't sense them somehow. Scarcely breathing, she heard the creature move on.

"That lady," Piotr said.

"*Please* don't talk," Katla whispered. "They might hear us." Assuming the Martians had ears, which the exobiologist in her couldn't state with any certainty. The creatures resembled, in a way, Earth crustaceans, which relied on sensory hairs to detect vibrations in their surrounding environment, be it water or air. It could be the Martians possessed a similar auditory system.

The issue became moot when a multifaceted eye at the end of a curving stalk came over the edge of the desk and stared right at them.

Captain Archard Rahn slapped in a new magazine and blasted a row of charging Martians. Private Everett added his own auto-fire. Between them, they dropped the things three-deep, and yet still the tide poured into the studio.

The broadcast crew lay all about them, gore everywhere.

"On me!" Archard cried, and backpedaled to a wall as far from the doors as they could get. "Frag rounds!" he warned, and banged off three grenades in succession, sweeping from left to right.

Tremendous blasts obliterated the doors and the creatures streaming through them.

Archard felt the concussive force even through his suit.

The stream of Martians lessened but didn't stop.

"Now you!" Archard commanded.

Private Everett imitated him exactly; three grenades, from left to right, fired so close together the three blasts were almost one.

More Martians were obliterated. Bits fell like raindrops.

Only a few were left standing, and they weaved and swayed as if confused.

Archard chopped them down with a spray of 5.56 mm. Finally, the last of them dropped.

Human and Martian body parts carpeted the floor. A few of the latter still moved, twitching weakly.

"Now what?" Everett said.

"On me." Archard made for the blistered doors, leaping over the fallen. He was so low on ammo, he didn't finish off the wounded Martians.

"What's that up above?" Everett said.

Archard heard it, too. A muffled crash, as if a section of roof had caved in. Or—and the thought sent a spike of consternation through him—something *on* the roof had toppled over. "No way," he said under his breath.

"Sir?"

They bounded out of the studio. Archard growling into his mic, "Pasco, can you hear me?"

"Sir!" crackled the metallic reply.

"Sitrep."

"The street is clear. Everything seems normal. You'd never know we're being attacked."

Archard's worst suspicion was being confirmed.

Pasco wasn't done. "I heard the shooting on the comm-link but stayed put like you told me."

"Good man," Archard said. "I want you on the maser. Cover us as we come out."

"You got it, sir."

The receptionist's body and arms and legs were near her desk, her ePad in shambles.

"I have a question, sir," Private Everett said between breaths.

"I'm listening."

"Why did the Martians hit the Broadcast Center? Was it coincidence? Or to cut off our communications?"

They reached the front doors and barreled outside. Stopping, Archard turned and looked up in time to see a relay tower tilt, then crash onto the roof. "Does that answer your question?"

"These critters are smarter than I reckoned."

"Let's hope they're not smarter than us," Archard said.

37

Levlin Winslow never could take pain. When he was a boy, any little scrape brought him to tears. To have his thumb broken was agony. He threw back his head and shrieked.

The Martians just stood there.

Winslow tried to pull free but the blue creature held fast. He jerked, and kicked, and whimpered. He stopped when the blue thing held him out toward the yellow Martian. Once again he was subjected to an intense scrutiny. He tried to pull away when the yellow creature reached out. He thought he was about to have his head ripped off. Instead, the yellow Martian lightly placed its fingers on his temples.

Nausea assailed him. His stomach flip-flopped. A prickly sensation, similar to a heat rash, spread down his entire body. Worst of all was a sickening feeling in his head, as if his brain was being poisoned. The chamber, and its occupants, spun and danced.

The yellow Martian touched him for a considerable while. Finally, it lowered its arms and turned to the blue creature. For several minutes they were motionless, although other Martians in the chamber moved quietly about.

Winslow was unprepared when the blue thing unexpectedly let go. He sprawled flat, hurting a wrist. Struggling to regain his senses, he sat up. His thumb throbbed. He would give anything for a pain med. "What did I do to deserve this?" he said to the basalt floor.

The four creatures that had brought him from New Meridian were suddenly next to him. He yipped in fright as they seized his arms and legs and hoisted him between them.

"What are you doing?" Winslow mewed.

Eyes waving, they scrabbled toward an opening across the way.

"Where are you taking me?" Winslow hoped it was a cell. He would try to set his thumb and pray, pray, pray that the U.N.I.C. came to his rescue.

The quartet bore him along dark passage after dark passage. He noticed that, weirdly, their eyes moved in synchrony. When one looked right, the others looked right. When one turned its eyes to look behind them, they all turned their eyes.

Winslow didn't try to figure out why. Nothing about the Martians made sense. Their physiologies, their minds, were too strange. They didn't have faces, or nostrils, or, now that he thought about it, mouths. They must have some way of eating, but he really didn't care. He just wanted out of there. He wanted to be home safe in New Meridian, and to get the hell off Mars on the next ship to Earth.

The four creatures veered into a chamber with a high ceiling, and halted.

Winslow was so astounded at what he saw, he barely noticed when they released him and he fell to the ground.

There were over a score of Martians in the chamber, a new kind. Umbrella-shaped carapaces topped four-meter tall bodies no thicker than Winslow's leg. Their eye stalks were short, barely a hand's-length. Some were clustered around various basalt bowls and benches, others moving about.

At Winslow's entrance, they stopped what they were doing, and turned. He saw that one of the things held a greyish object that it was about to place into a wide bowl filled with a viscous green fluid.

"What in the world?" Winslow gasped.

Rock shelves lined the walls on either side. He glanced over, and his mind reeled. On the nearest shelves were rows of human heads. Heads he recognized as fellow colonists from New Meridian.

Winslow screamed.

The four creatures that had brought him pounced. He was too terrified to resist as they pinned him on his back with his arms and legs spread-eagle.

One of the new kind approached. Its umbrella-shaped carapace bent and its eyes regarded Winslow.

"You don't want to do this!" Winslow sobbed. "I'm important, I tell you. My government will trade for me. Whatever you want."

The Martian's rock-hard fingers closed on his neck.

"Please! No!"

Winslow experienced a tearing sensation, and dark drops flew past his eyes. He tried to speak, to plead for his life, but his throat and mouth were filled with warm liquid.

Blackness descended. So did total silence. Strangely, Winslow felt as if cool air were on his skin, yet he couldn't feel the rest of his body. He was conscious of movement, and then the strangest thing of all occurred. A faint green light enveloped him, and for some reason, he felt wet.

38

Katla Dkany broke out in gooseflesh.

A second eye appeared next to the first. The twin stalks separated, one eye moving right, the left, then came together again.

Katla tensed to make a break for it. Before she could move, Piotr lunged and grabbed a stalk. With a sharp outcry, he squeezed and yanked.

The Martian's grippers lashed down and seized the boy's wrist.

"No!" Katla shouted as Piotr was torn from her grasp. Darting out from under the desk, she turned.

The Martian was poised on top of it, holding Piotr at arm's length. Piotr had let go of the stalk and both of the eyes were roving up and down his body. The creature seemed more curious than angry.

"Don't hurt him!" Katla said. "He's just a child, damn you."

An eye swiveled toward her and back to Piotr.

Katla's intuition screamed that something dreadful was about to happen. She cast about for a weapon and spied an antique snow globe on the desk. She remembered that it belonged to Sharon's great grandmother, and that Sharon brought it to Mars because it reminded her of her family back on Earth. Snatching it up, she struck with all her strength at the only part of the Martian she might be able to hurt: an eye.

The Martian dropped Piotr and exploded backward off the desk, landing meters away. Its whole body shook and its eyes waved wildly about.

"So you can be hurt!" Katla gloated, but her elation was short-lived.

The creature stopped quaking and turned its eyes on them. Its rock-hard digits opened and closed menacingly.

Grabbing Piotr, Katla retreated until her back was pressed to the wall. She had nowhere else to go. If she went around the desk, the Martian would be on them in a heartbeat.

Piotr pressed close and said in her ear, "I don't want to die."

Neither did Katla. She still had the snow globe. It wasn't much but it would have to do, and she raised it, prepared to fight.

The Martian sprang. Simultaneously, a burst of auto-fire rang out. Leaden hail smashed the creature to the floor.

Framed in the light of the hospital entrance was a soldier in a military EVA suit, his weapon trained on the Martian.

"Archard!" Katla exclaimed in relief.

He came toward them, and Katla flew around the desk, spreading her arm to embrace him. "Oh, Archard!" To her amazement, he pushed her aside and stepped in front of her as if to shield her with his body. Then she saw why.

More of the creatures were scrambling out of the former blood pressure patient's room.

"On the floor!" Archard shouted, and his finger flicked on his weapon.

Katla barely flattened when an explosion rocked the hall. Most of the Martians were blown apart, but not all, and more were streaming from the room after them.

"To the doors," Archard yelled, "but stay close!"

Katla understood. Heaving upright, she kept an arm against his broad back.

Archard sent burst after burst into the Martians but still they came.

Katla envisioned being overwhelmed and torn to pieces.

Another soldier charged through the entrance, his own weapon blazing. Between them, the onslaught momentarily stopped. Instantly, Archard turned to the newcomer, whom Katla recognized as Private Everett.

"Get them into the tank!"

"Sir!"

Katla had nearly forgotten that the lesser Martian gravity enabled humans to perform feats they couldn't on Earth. Such as now, as Everett plucked her and Piotr up in one arm and bore her out of the hospital with an ease and speed he never could back home.

She breathed easier when she was in the military's rover, and Everett, with a kindly smile, lowered her and Piotr onto a seat.

"Good to see you again, kid."

A third trooper, Private Pasco, was manning their turret gun. He hollered, "Here they come!" and there was a low thrumming followed by a series of sizzling sounds that made Katla think of bacon frying in a pan.

Pasco yipped with glee and yelled, "Take that, you ugly suckers!"

Archard hastened in. He slapped the large button that closed the bay door and came over. Gently reaching out, he touched her chin, a rare display for him. "Thank God we got to you in time."

"Where do we go? What do we do?" Katla asked. More importantly, "How can we stop these things from overrunning the colony?"

Archard did something else that was rare for him. He worriedly looked her in the eyes and admitted, "I don't know that we can."

39

Archard was caught between the proverbial rock and a hard place. To go rushing around New Meridian searching for Martians was pointless. He didn't have enough men to withstand an all-out assault. Not when the Martians could break in from underground anywhere they wanted. It was grimly ironic that the colony's defenses had been breached by an attack from the one direction the experts never expected an attack to come from.

He needed time to strategize. "Headquarters, and step on it."

"What about me, sir?" Private Pasco asked from the turret.

"Stay where you are. Burn any Martians you see."

"With pleasure."

Archard wearily sank into the front passenger seat. He had been on the go for so long it was taking a toll. Shrugging the fatigue off, he tried, yet again, to raise Wellsville and Bradbury. Predictably, neither answered.

"Look yonder, sir," Private Everett said.

The tank was turning onto another street. Bathed in its headlights, a torso on its back with the arms and legs placed to either side. Otherwise, the street was empty.

"Wonder who it was," Everett said.

"Keep going," Archard directed. By rights, they should identify every victim, but that would have to wait. *If* they survived the night, *if* they drove the Martians out, and *if* they could secure the colony, then, and only then, would they take up the task of identifying the dead.

Archard boosted the audio but he didn't pick up so much as a hint that anything out of the ordinary was taking place.

"It's too quiet," Everett said. "Could they have killed everybody already?"

Archard doubted it. More likely, the colonists were doing as he had instructed and were holed up in their habitats. He wished the tank had been fitted with side-scan radar. In common military and police use on Earth, it could see through walls. So far as he knew, only the U.N.I.C. squad at Bradbury had one. More cost-cutting by the bean counters.

The tank made another turn. More lights glowed in the windows of several homes.

Archard took that as a good sign. There *were* colonists left, and it was his duty to save them.

As if Private Everett was reading his thoughts, he said, "What are we going to do, sir? There aren't enough rovers to evacuate everyone. Even if there were, we'd never reach the other colonies."

Up in the turret, Private Pasco remarked, "We have to kill the Martians. That's the only way."

"All of them?" Everett said skeptically. "The captain says there are thousands of the things."

"For all I know," Archard said, "there are millions."

Pasco said out of the blue, "I guess one of us will have to put the RAM 3000 to the test."

Archard had been thinking along the same lines but had kept it to himself for the time being.

"I officially volunteer," Everett said, with a hopeful glance at Archard. "In that baby, I could kill Martians like there's no tomorrow."

Katla cleared her throat. "Pardon my ignorance, but what's the RAM 3000?"

"A battle suit," Archer enlightened her. "The latest in a line of combat armor that stretches back a century and a half. Specifically designed for use on Mars."

"What does it do?" Katla asked.

Private Everett laughed. "Ma'am, that baby turns your average grunt into a one-man army."

"I've never heard of it," Katla said. "Has it been used a lot in war?"

"Well, actually, no," Everett said. "We haven't had any wars up here to fight."

Katla stared pointedly at Archard. "So whoever puts it on to hunt the Martians down doesn't really know if it will perform as it should?"

Everett shrugged. "I suppose that's one way of looking at it."

"There's another?"

"Sure," the Kentuckian said, and laughed. "For the fun of kicking Martian ass."

40

The United Nations Interplanetary Corps headquarters building in New Meridian had three levels.

On the upper floor were their personal quarters. Each trooper was assigned a room, a luxury in the U.N.I.C., since on Earth single soldiers lived in barracks. The behavioral scientists had insisted it was better for morale. A common kitchen and entertainment area were also provided.

The ground floor consisted of Archard's office, a ready room, the motor pool that housed the tank, and a state-of-the-art gym with aerobic machine, weights, and more. Keeping fit on Mars required more effort than on Earth. Mars' lower gravity weakened human muscle mass and bone density and adversely affected the circulatory system. In order to stay at peak health, a daily exercise regimen was required.

HQ's sublevel served as storage. Extra weapons, ammunition, arms they didn't ordinarily use, and other special equipment were kept under lock and key.

In a large room with its own airlock access to the surface via a ramp, the RAM 3000 hung suspended off the floor in a reinforced frame. The battle suit weighed over a ton. It was powered by a miniature version of the EDM propulsion system that enabled spacecraft to travel from Earth to Mars in an eighth of the time it took using conventional rocketry.

RAM was an acronym for Robotic Armored Man-of-War. Nearly four meters high and three meters wide at the shoulders, it brought to mind a gigantic suit of medieval armor. Essentially, it was a massive, reinforced exoskeleton, bristling with armaments. To gain access, the operator opened the chest cavity and slid down in.

Archard placed a hand on a huge boot and looked up at the oversized helmet. The RAM was touted as the most lethal killing machine ever invented. He could only hope that the big brains who designed it knew what they were doing.

"Merciful heavens." Katla Dkany was gaping in amazement. Beside her, his hand in hers, Piotr stood stupefied. "I had no idea."

Private Everett had climbed a ladder so he could reach the chest plate and was going through the mandated systems check. "So far all the readings are green, sir."

Private Pasco was glued to an eReader, paging through one of the RAM's tech manuals. "I found what you wanted, Captain."

"Let me hear it," Archard said.

"The operational range varies according to power consumption." Pasco recited. "At full power under combat conditions the range is estimated—"

"Estimated?" Archard interrupted.

"That's what it says, sir," Pasco confirmed, and continued. "At full power under combat conditions, the range is estimated to be two hundred kilometers. To extend the range, it is recommended that lower power settings be used. At half power, the Robotic Armored Man-of-War should have a range of four to five hundred kilometers." Pasco stopped reading.

"That's all?"

"Yes, sir."

"No mention of how far the suit can go at its lowest setting under non-combat conditions?"

Pasco consulted the manual again, then looked up, confused. "No, sir. I don't get it, though. Non-combat conditions? Why does that matter?"

"It might," Archard said. He didn't elaborate. But a germ of an idea had taken root.

Up on the ladder, Private Everett called down, "Systems check completed. You're good to go, sir."

Rungs on the frame enabled Archard to climb high enough to turn his back to the suit and ease into the chest opening. There was minimal cushioning. Comfort wasn't the main consideration.

Once he was in, Archard lowered the helmet. The controls were voice activated. He said simply, "Power up", and the RAM came to life. He told the inboard computer to close the chest plate, and once he was sealed in, he flexed the RAM's fingers, getting the feel.

Private Everett, meanwhile, had descended the ladder and rolled it away and was now activating the winch that would lower the heavy frame to the floor.

Private Pasco went to the airlock panel and waited to open it.

Archard felt a slight jar as the RAM's boots thumped the floor. He scanned the helmet holo display, familiarizing himself. He'd only used the RAM once, briefly, as part of training.

Everett disengaged the frame and swung it aside. "You're free and clear, Captain."

Archard lifted one foot and then the other. All systems were indeed functioning. He looked down at Katla and their eyes met. Then he carefully turned, the RAM thunking with each step.

"Let's do this."

41

The moment Archard was out of the airlock, he powered up the EDM drive, kicked in the thrusters on his back, and went airborne. In a few giddy blinks of an eye, he was hovering near the top of the dome. The thrusters weren't entirely silent; even in stealth mode they made a slight hiss. He didn't care if the Martians heard him. Let them come. He was in the RAM for one reason and one reason only—to kill every Martian he could.

Archard held his arms out to either side and looked down at the giant exoskeleton in which he was encased. He raised his left knee and lowered it, then his right knee, and marveled at the ease with which the RAM responded. It didn't feel like more than a ton. It felt no heavier than a set of winter clothes, except for the boots. They were reinforced to bear the RAM's weight, and comparatively speaking, felt three to four times heavier than regular boots would.

Archard turned his attention to the holo display, which was projected in the space between his face and the helmet's faceplate. He could look right through the readings, and out the helmet. The first time he'd used the RAM it had been distracting, initially. But he'd quickly gotten used to switching from close up to far away. He did it a number of times now to acclimatize himself.

Next, on visual, he ran through the entire electromagnetic spectrum. He hiked the audio sensors, too. Not surprisingly, the colony appeared perfectly peaceful.

Archard had one last system check and then he could get to it. "Private Everett, do you read me?"

"Affirmative, sir."

"Prep the tank, as I instructed. The extra food, the extra water, everything."

"Will do."

"Maintain radio silence until further notice." Archard very much doubted the Martians could listen in, or that they could understand human speech if they did.

Increasing power to the thrusters, Archard flew in a small practice loop. They took some getting used to, like the throttle on a motorcycle. Too much power, and he might tumble out of control. The RAM responded superbly.

Archard made for the Broadcast Center. The last he'd seen, Martians were up on the roof, destroying everything. Two hundred meters out, he slowed until he seemed to be floating.

The dishes, the towers, the arrays, had all been demolished.

Disrupting enemy communications was a basic military tactic. It set Archard to wondering why the Martians hadn't thought to attack the Atmosphere Center, as well. In one fell swoop they could wipe out the colony. Could it be the Martians didn't recognize the Atmosphere Center's importance? Or was there a more sinister reason at work?

His musing was cut short by the patter of running feet and a shriek of mortal terror.

Archard locked on the glowing holo image of a woman with a child in her arms fleeing down a street, and boosted power. His motion sensors told him that 'something' was after them, but once again the Martians failed to register as discreet heat signatures.

In seconds, he was over the woman. He heard her panting and the child whimper.

Six Martians scuttled in pursuit.

"Help us!" the mother shouted to the empty buildings she was passing. "Help us, please!"

It struck Archard that the Martians weren't moving as fast as they could, which suggested they were deliberating hanging back, perhaps so the woman would lead them to more humans.

Archard came down fast and hard between the creatures and their quarry, spreading his legs and using his left arm to lessen the impact.

Abruptly stopping, the Martians raised their stalk eyes. The RAM was something they hadn't seen before, and they studied it, as was their habit.

"Keep running," Archard boomed at the woman without turning his head. "Get to safety." He didn't look to see if she obeyed.

Pointing his left arm, he was about to unleash a weapon but changed his mind. The RAM was supposed to be practically impervious to a physical assault. Now was as good a time as any to put that to test.

Bunching the battle suit's enormous fists, Archard plowed into the Martians. One ran up his leg almost to his waist and he brought his fists together, reducing the creature to pulp. He punched another that jumped at his chest, splitting it open. Two others attacked from either side. He grabbed the quickest by a leg and swung it against the other and both dropped in pieces.

That left two. The nearest sprang at his helmet. Catching it as if it were a ball, he tore the thing in half.

Archard laughed in sheer savage joy. The feeling of raw power was intoxicating. The creatures had hardly touched him, and there was only one left.

To his surprise, the survivor was fleeing back down the street.

Raising his arm, Archard keyed in a dart.

The creature was a block away and moving like a bat out of Hades when Archard fired. The RAM's in-board targeting was spot-on. The dart struck the Martian in the center of its body mass and broke into a hundred tiny flechettes that ripped through the creature like so many razors. The thing crashed down, riddled.

Surveying the slaughter, Archard nodded in satisfaction. He was on the verge of taking to the air to go find more Martians when a timid voice stopped him.

"Mister? Can you hear me in there?"

42

She was young, in her late twenties, her long black hair disheveled from her flight. "I thought we were dead. What are those things?"

Archard had met her a couple of times. "Trisna, isn't it? Trisna Sahir? From New Delhi?"

"That's me," Trisna said, and indicated her daughter, who was clinging to her neck. "This is Behula." She rose onto the tips of her toes, the better to see his helmet. "Captain Rahn, isn't it?"

"Yes. Remind me where you work again."

"The Supply Center. In Dispersals." Trisna regarded the dead Martians. "Behula and I, we like to take walks at night and gaze at the stars. Tonight we ran into those things." She shivered and held her daughter closer.

"You didn't hear my warning?"

"What warning?"

Archard wondered how many others hadn't heard. "I'll explain on the way." Bending at the knees, he beckoned, then lowered the RAM's arms to ground level.

"What are you doing?" Trisna said.

"Climb on."

"Excuse me?"

"There are a lot more of those things loose in the colony. I need to take you and your daughter to U.N.I.C. headquarters so I can get out and help others like you."

Moving as if she were walking on glass, Trisna brought Behula over. She set her daughter on top of his right arm, climbed up, then cradled Behula while stretching her legs over his other arm.

"Hold on," Archard cautioned, and slowly rose a couple of meters into the air.

Trisna gasped, and the girl cried out.

"You're perfectly safe," Archard assured them. "I won't drop you." Still, he didn't rise any higher. Gradually accelerating, he contacted Private Everett and related the latest.

"How many people have these horrible things killed?" Trisna asked when he was done.

"I don't know," Archard said. "I hope to round up as many survivors as I can."

"You'll have to go door to door, won't you?" Trisna said. "That could take forever. With those awful things ready to attack you at any time."

"I handled those," Archard said. But she had a point. Even in the RAM, it would take hours to search the entire colony. And the suit was so huge, he couldn't enter any of the house modules; he wouldn't fit through the doors or airlocks.

"It's too bad you can't do as we had to in India," Trisna said. "You might have heard. We had a monkey problem. Millions overran our cities. We couldn't kill them because, you know, we're Hindu. The government tried catching them but monkeys are clever little buggers. So they hired special workers to lure the monkeys away. It's unfortunate you can't do the same, yes?"

"Yes," Archard said, as the seed of a new idea took root.

The ready room at U.N.I.C. headquarters was small but had twelve chairs, enough for the meeting Archard had called. He stood at the front of the room, his arms crossed. "Input?"

"Are you sure about this, sir?" Private Pasco said. "What if it doesn't work?"

Archard had detailed his plan to the two troopers and the women. Katla and Trisna were civilians but their lives were at stake and they had a right to offer their opinions. "Then we're no worse off than we already are."

"Except we could lose you," Private Everett said.

"Yes," Katla quietly interjected. "There's that." Her eyes were pools of worry. "Realistically, what are your chances of making it out alive?"

Archard shrugged. "The important thing is to lure the Martians out of New Meridian and give Everett and Pasco time to go door to door."

"The search will go faster if the doctor and I help," Trisna said. Her daughter was perched on her knees. "I want to, and I'm sure Dr. Dkany feels the same."

Katla nodded.

"Begging your pardon, ma'am," Everett said, "but it's too dangerous. You ladies should stay here where it's safe."

"For how long?" Trisna said. "Based on what Captain Rahn told us, unless something drastic is done, the colony will soon be overrun. Or am I wrong?" She stared at Archard.

"The RAM can only hold the Martians off for so long," Archard said. He might kill hundreds, even thousands, but in the end, he'd expend all the suit's armaments, and they would be at the Martians' mercy.

"Something else to think about," Katla said. "It's only a matter of time before the Martians think to hit the Atmosphere Center. When that goes down, we're all dead."

"They haven't yet," Pasco said. "Maybe they're not that bright."

"Or maybe they have a reason for not wiping us all out," Katla said.

Archard spoke up. "Whether they hit the A. C. or cause a breach that sucks out all the air, the result will be the same." He shook his head. "No, my plan is best. We must evacuate New Meridian. To do that, we need to lure the Martians away. I can think of only one way to do that."

"And if you don't come back?" Private Everett bluntly asked.

"You resort to Plan B," Archard said. "Gather up all the survivors you can find and take them to the farm farthest from the volcano. Use the tank and every rover in the colony. You might have to make two or three trips but get it done. Then wait to be rescued. Someone is bound to come from the other colonies, eventually."

"We hope," Pasco said.

Katla surprised Archard by coming up and placing her hand on his arm. "I know better than to try and talk you out of this. Don't let those things kill you."

"I'll try my best," Archard said.

43

The stars were brighter outside the dome. In Mars' rarefied atmosphere, they gleamed like diadems in a celestial crown.

Archard would need every bit of power the RAM could muster when he reached his destination, so for the moment he didn't engage the thrusters. In incredible leaps, he traveled to a point two hundred meters due north of New Meridian.

Planting the line of sensors was easy. He simply shoved the spikes they were attached to into the ground. To counter the jamming, which he had yet to account for, he set up a portable relay that amplified the sensors' signals. He tapped the button for the test circuit, and the signal light glowed. "Everett, are you reading these?"

"Affirmative, sir."

"I'm on my way."

"Good luck, sir."

Archard turned his faceplate to the heavens and activated the thrusters. The RAM swept so swiftly into the sky, it was breathtaking. Speed was essential. Any time now, the Martians inside the dome could penetrate U.N.I.C. headquarters.

At full power, Archard streaked across the Martian sky, a human meteor out for vengeance. He had a GPS lock on Albor Tholus, and in less than ten minutes he arced in over the towering cone. Slowing, he hovered and peered electronically into the volcano's foreboding depths.

Archard was about to take the fight to the Martians. It was his hope, his prayer, that a direct assault on their underground warren would cause the creatures in New Meridian to rush to the aid of their crustoid brethren. He was the lure that would draw the things out, and hopefully buy Everett and the others the time they needed to complete their search.

"So where are you?" Archard said aloud. The RAM registered no life at all. Small wonder the orbiting satellites hadn't, either.

Archard wished he had a nuke. That would be the easy away. Drop one in and get the hell out, and goodbye Martians. But the brass hadn't seen any need for nukes on Mars.

Archard clicked his comm-link. "HQ, this is Captain Rahn. Do you read me?" Static crackled in his earphones. "Of course not," he said, and got down to business.

The RAM'S life support system was green, all weapons systems were green, the power bar had barely gone down. The battle suit was as ready as it was ever going to be.

Archard took a deep breath and slowly let it out. Some would say he was about to commit suicide, that he didn't stand a snowball's chance in hell of descending into the dark heart of the Martian enclave and making it out alive. If so, so be it. This was the only way he could think of to save as many colonists as possible.

Archard thought of his parents back on Earth, he thought of his sister, happily married, and her kids. He remembered, of all things, a dog he'd had as a boy, and how much he'd loved that mutt.

Shaking himself, Archard tilted the thrusters and gained speed. The caldera expanded until it was a giant maw spread wide to devour him.

A lone speck in the middle of the thirty-kilometer hole, Archard swooped into the bowels of the Martian underground. Down, and down, and down even more. A kilometer. A kilometer and a half. Two.

The walls of the caldera flared outward to become the roof of the vast cavern.

Below, a legion of alien adversaries were going about their regular routines. He'd caught them completely by surprise.

"Our turn, you bastards," Archard declared, and dived to the attack. Cleaving the air at full power, he hurtled at a broad walkway crowded with creatures. The RAM struck with the force of a cannonball. The walkway was basalt, as hard as iron, but not even iron could withstand over a ton of brutal impact from a metal ten times harder. The walkway shattered, raining debris, and Martians.

Arcing up and around, Archard spied a high tower with arched doorways and windows. A lot of Martians were going in and out.

Zeroing in, he let fly with a missile from a forearm gauntlet. Like an arrow from a bow, it flashed across the intervening space. The blast enveloped the entire tower in a billowing ball of fire.

To his left and slightly below, a squat structure sat on a wide shelf. Drawn by the fireball, Martians by the score rushed out, their stalks waving wildly.

Banking, Archard opened up with the RAM's M537 Minigun. At a cyclic rate of five thousand rounds a minute, the lead chewed through the creatures like hot nails through butter. Shredded Martians pitched over the shelf or fell where they stood.

By now, the entire beehive had awakened to his attack, and nearly every Martian in sight had stopped what they were doing to fix their multifaceted eyes on the RAM.

Archard couldn't resist; he bellowed in fierce glee and dived toward the largest building in sight, a virtual basalt castle half a kilometer lower. He reasoned that the bigger the structure, the more important it must be, and the more likely that it contained the Martians' leaders.

Creatures poured from within. The reddish round ones, the larger blue ones. On a balcony appeared something new; a yellow being three meters high, the only one of its kind he had seen so far.

Archard resorted to the RAM'S ion cannon. His first beam cut the yellow creature in half. His next reduced a dozen Martians to severed wrecks. Pirouetting up and away to gain distance, he selected a Penetrator, the most devastating missile in the RAM's arsenal, centered the holo's crosshairs on the castle, and said, "Fire."

Designed with a top speed of fifteen thousand kilometers per hour, the Penetrator was almost too fast for the human eye to follow. It hit exactly where the computer told it to hit. An artificial sun lit the cavern, a blinding-white nova that atomized the castle and everything around it.

Archard neglected to brace for the shock wave and paid for his mistake by tumbling helmet over boots for a good fifty meters. When he came to a stop, he righted the RAM and scoured his vicinity for more targets. He mustn't give the Martians a moment's respite. The more destruction he caused, the more likely the

Martians in New Meridian would be compelled to come to their aid.

His major advantage was flight. He could wreak havoc immune from retaliation. Or so he assumed until he happened to look down.

Another new kind of Martians had appeared, and these could fly. A whole swarm of them was rising toward him.

44

Dr. Katla Dkany stood behind the two soldiers, holding Piotr. Trisna was beside her with Behula. Both children had fallen asleep. Katla was thankful for that. They had been through harrowing ordeals, Piotr in particular. And the sad part was, their ordeals weren't over.

"Come on, come on," the trooper from Kentucky was saying. He and the Spaniard were glued to a console in the command center.

"Please keep your voice down," Trisna said quietly.

Private Everett glanced at her and went to reply, then looked at Behula and at Piotr, and turned back to the radio. "Sure, lady," he said, not as loudly.

"The captain should be at the volcano by now," Private Pasco said. "We should know soon."

"Keep everything crossed," Private Everett said.

"I'm glad I'm not the pessimist you are," Pasco said, and beamed. "My mother always said I am an optimist at heart."

"Yeah, well," Everett said, "where I come from, an optimist is somebody who goes through life with blinders on."

"Blinders?"

"Like a horse."

"People aren't horses."

"You'd think," Everett said, and stiffened. "Look! Motion readings. A lot of them."

Pasco thrust his chin over Everett's shoulder. "It's working. The things are leaving the colony. They're heading for the volcano, just like the captain predicted they would."

"We can begin the search," Trisna said. She didn't sound happy at the prospect.

"We'll wait a few minutes to be sure all the Martians are gone," Everett said.

"Some might not leave," Katla felt it necessary to mention.

"That is my worry," Trisna said.

Everett swiveled in his chair. "Ladies, you don't have to help. You can stay in the tank with your kids."

"No," Katla said. "I told Archard I would, and I will."

"I, as well," Trisna said.

"Suit yourselves," Everett said. "But the kids don't leave the tank for any reason. Are you okay with that?"

"Mustn't they?" Trisna said.

"You can't fight with your girl in your arms," Everett said. "We're issuing each of you a weapon. In fact, let's do that right now. I'll show you how to use them."

Katla was surprised at how light the ICW felt. Everett explained that a microchip controlled the various functions. He showed them the selector settings, and warned them not to shoot a fragmentation grenade unless they were a good thirty meters from the target. The killing radius was fifteen meters; the extra margin was to be safe.

"I don't know if I can do this," Trisna said, regarding her weapon with a troubled expression. "Take life, I mean."

Everett chuckled. "Alien life doesn't hardly count, ma'am."

"I am Hindu. To us, all life counts. Even the life of those strange creatures."

"Fine. Then do nothing and let them kill you and your daughter."

"That was harsh," Katla said.

"No. He is right," Trisna said. "I must decide. Which is more important? Behula? Or the lives of these beings?"

They 'saddled up,' as Everett put it.

Katla gently placed Piotr on blankets that Pasco had spread out, with a cushion for a pillow. Trisna eased Behula down next to him. The girl stirred, but neither woke up.

"They look so peaceful," Trisna said. "So precious."

Private Everett drove up a ramp and turned right onto Sagan Street. In the passenger seat, Private Pasco was running his fingers over the holo, moving symbols around.

"No motion whatsoever anywhere within range."

"So far, so good." Everett braked in front of a house module. Light glowed in windows covered by closed curtains. "We'll check this one. Ladies, you'll accompany us, if you please. Watch how we do it. Then you do the same when we split up."

Katla was impressed at how efficient the soldiers were. They approached the door from either side, their weapons to their shoulders. Pasco covered while Everett entered an override code. As the door opened, Everett quickly stepped back and raised his ICW. He nodded at Pasco, then poked his head in and looked both ways. Darting inside, he crouched. Pasco did likewise, facing the other way. They stayed like that a bit, then Everett said in an odd tone, "All clear, ladies. But brace yourselves."

There was a hole in the living room floor. Around it, in an almost dry pool of scarlet, lay the bodies and limbs of the family who lived there. But not their heads.

"Well, damn," Everett said. "We're off to a good start."

Incredulous, Archard hovered above the rising swarm. They were a half kilometer below, ascending rapidly.

The RAM distinguished fifty-six distinct targets, its holo crosshairs flashing from one to the next with lightning rapidity.

Switching to telescopic, Archard scrutinized the flyers in minute detail. They were black, their eyes inset into a ridge at the front of their carapace. Instead of the usual eight legs, they had eight pairs of short wings, wings so stubby, it seemed impossible the creatures could fly. Yet they did, their wings vibrating at tremendous speed, similar to hummingbirds. Their forelimbs were folded close to their bodies, with spike-like protrusions at the end.

Archard arced down, clenched the RAM's fists, and amped his thrusters. He didn't engage his armaments. He needed his missiles for after. These things, he would take on hand-to-hand.

Air whistled past his helmet. He heard, too, the low-pitched buzzing of the creatures' wings.

A big one out in front rose to meet him.

"Fine," Archard growled, and slammed into it going full-bore. His fists caved its carapace as if it were putty. He smashed into another, and a third, and hardly felt the impacts.

The rest converged.

Archard punched and kicked and swatted, smashing the flyers right and left. That heady sense of raw power came over him again, stronger than before. He banked and pulverized several foes, spun and crushed another.

They were all around him.

Tilting his head and spreading his arms wide, Archard soared clear. Or tried to. They were on him in a black cloud of wings and spikes. He drove a fist into one, backhanded a second. Several tried to seize his legs but he kicked them loose.

Spikes speared at his chest, his arms, his shoulders, his helmet.

Suddenly he was in trouble. There were too many. Most of their blows glanced off his armor but more than a few dented it. All it would take was a single large rupture, and he was done for.

Fists flailing, Archard fought in a fury. His decision to go hand-to-hand might not have been wise. He executed a spin-kick and cleared enough space to do what he probably should have done in the first place. He ignited the RAM's flamethrower.

Half a dozen flyers were incinerated. The rest scattered as if in a panic. They went a short way and swung around, staring. It was as if they had never encountered fire.

Archard didn't bother to wonder how that could be. He seized the initiative, his flamethrower roaring. Again the creatures scattered. Again they formed a ring around him.

Archard could take a hint. He switched to the Minigun and poured lead into their buzzing ranks, turning in a circle as he went.

Flyers dropped in droves.

Only a few were left when Archard's helmet was struck a tremendous blow from behind, and the cavernous world around him went dark.

45

At the next house, it was the same. A family of six had been slaughtered, their remains neatly arranged in what Katla took to be some sort of ritual. A troubling insight in that it opened a Pandora's box of possibilities. Katla realized she must think outside her own mental box, and not dismiss the creatures as animals.

"Why do they take the heads?" Private Pasco said to no one in particular.

"Beats the hell out of me," Private Everett said. "Maybe they like to eat brains."

Trisna had averted her eyes from the gore. "Please. Don't make it worse by joking about it."

"Who's joking?" Everett replied.

"Let's move on," Katla said. "We should separate, as Archard wanted, to cover more ground."

"We'll do one more together," Everett overrode her. "To be sure you have it down." He gave Trisna a troubled glance. "Are you up to this?"

Trisna caught the look. "You need not worry about me."

The next building was an apartment complex for singles. Built to resemble an apartment on Earth, it was three-stories high. The lobby was small, and empty. Since anyone could come and go as they pleased, there was no need for a desk clerk. This was Mars, not an inner city rampant with crime on Earth.

The first apartment, Everett and Pasco did their entry routine. The Spaniard poked his head in first and promptly jerked it out again, paling.

"Dios, en el cielo!"

Everett took a look, and swore. "Wait here, ladies," he whispered. With a motion at Pasco, both darted inside.

Trisna turned and gazed out the front doors in the direction of the tank.

"Worried about your daughter?" Katla said.

"Aren't you, about your son?"

"He's not mine, but yes," Katla said. "They'll be all right. They're safe in the tank. The soldiers were in a fight with a lot of Martians earlier today, and the Martians couldn't get inside."

"Perhaps the Martians weren't trying."

Katla was beginning to understand why Private Everett was so concerned about her.

Just then the Kentuckian appeared in the doorway. "Ladies, you should come take a look. We're up against something new."

Most of the living room floor was now a hole many times the size of previous entry points.

"What could have made that?" Trisna said, aghast.

"Maybe the small ones have a daddy," Everett said.

"You joke about everything."

Katla peered into the black pit. To her immense relief, nothing moved. Whatever made it was gone.

"Let's back out," Everett said. "We don't want to push our luck."

Private Pasco went to the lift. A light on the panel indicated it was on the second floor. He pressed the button to bring it down. "How do they know?"

"Eh?" Everett said.

"How do the Martians know which buildings people are in?"

Everett shrugged. "Could be they're digging into all of them."

"We should check."

"What difference does it make?" Everett looked up. "What's keeping that thing?"

The second-floor indicator was still lit.

"I'm just saying maybe they can sense us somehow," Pasco said. "Even inside buildings."

"You ask me, you're giving them more credit than..." Private Everett got no further.

From above came a resounding crash, as if the building were about to collapse.

Archard snapped to full consciousness. He had only been out a minute or so. The RAM, as it was designed to, had absorbed most of the blow. He spun, seeking the source, and was startled to discover that in the heat of combat he had inadvertently descended to within a stone's-throw of a basalt bridge crowded with Martians.

Closest loomed a specimen of the large blue variety. Nine meters long and five meters high, it possessed a carapace as broad as the tank, and a segmented tail. Its arms, if they could be called that, were as thick as the RAM's.

Even as Archard watched, its many-faceted eyes did something he didn't know they could do. The stalks withdrew into small holes, nestling the eyes in protective niches.

"Prepping for combat?" Archard guessed.

Gripping the edge of the bridge, the blue Martian demonstrated prodigious strength by ripping off a jagged section of basalt. Raising it aloft, the creature poised on the brink.

Archard realized what had struck him the first time, He dropped a few meters just as the blue Martian threw the makeshift projectile, and the rock passed over his helmet.

Archard could end the clash then and there. One missile or dart would do the job.

Then the Martian did an astonishing thing; it gestured with its grippers, beckoning, as if challenging him to personal combat.

Archard kicked in the RAM'S thrusters and struck like a battering ram. For the flyers and the smaller Martians, that would have been enough to crumple them in death. The blue creature was tougher. It was knocked back but its carapace didn't rupture.

Archard closed with the thing. He blocked a stab at his faceplate and retaliated with a powerful jab between the creature's eyes. The blue Martian seized his wrist. He tried to pull away but the thing's grip was a vise. He drove his free fist at the arm holding him, only to have his other wrist seized.

Archard struggled to wrest loose. He'd almost succeeded when the Martian whipped its body around and slammed its segmented tail against the RAM's legs. The battle suit was supposed to be virtually immovable when its boots were firmly planted, but to Archard's dismay, his legs were swept out from under him and he crashed onto his back.

Still holding his wrists, the creature sprang on top of the RAM.

Archard bucked, or tried to. The RAM couldn't quite imitate the movement. It rose a little off the basalt, but not enough to dislodge his attacker. The thing pinned his arms, its carapace pressed to his chest. Its eye-stalks slid out of their holes, bringing its eyes close to his faceplate. He could have breathed on them if he wasn't wearing the helmet.

The RAM's motion sensors blared like klaxons. Scores of Martians were sweeping to the blue creature's aid. En masse, they would bury the RAM, and render escape impossible.

In desperation, Archard tried another tactic. Instead of bucking and pushing, he rolled, taking the blue Martian with him. The moment his back was off the basalt, he keyed a short burst from the thrusters. He thought it would break the creature's grip. Instead, they both pitched over the side.

46

Certain the ceiling was about to collapse, Katla threw herself against a wall, an arm raised to shield her head.

Trisna screamed and dropped to the floor.

The crash faded and rumbling ensued. It lasted perhaps a minute, dwindling into silence.

Katla started to straighten when a second crash boomed louder than the first.

Private Everett threw an arm around Pasco and propelled them both away from the elevator tube. "Look out!" he hollered.

The lift crashed down like a bomb. Glass that was supposed to be shatterproof, wasn't. Shards flew every which way, and a piece as long as a scalpel struck the wall centimeters from Katla's ear.

Trisna cried out. Not from fear, but from the pain of a thin piece of glass slicing into her thigh. Grabbing her leg, she clenched her jaw and said something in Hindu.

Private Everett recovered first. Springing erect, he helped Private Pasco to stand.

"That was close, buddy."

"What could have caused that?" Paso said in bewilderment.

"A cut cable, maybe." Everett moved to Trisna. "Let us have a look at that."

The soldiers helped Trisna to sit up, and Katla examined the wound. It wasn't life-threatening but, "She'll need stitches. There's a med-kit in the tank. I can extract it there."

Trisna exhaled loudly through her nose. "I'd rather the children didn't see. Can't you take the glass out now?"

"Not without the med kit," Katla insisted. "There's no telling how badly you'll bleed."

"Please. Behula has seen enough terrible things today."

"Ladies, this isn't a debate," Everett said. He was covering them. "We'll do it in the tank like the doc wants, and that's that."

"I'm not allowed to express my wishes?" Trisna said.

"Express them all you want," Everett said. "But we do what's best for everybody, not just your kid."

"You are cruel," Trisna said.

"Don't be angry," Pasco said to her. "We're only looking out for you."

"And we've jabbered enough," Everett said. He stepped to the tube and peered up it. "Whatever caused this might still be up there. Pasco and me should go see." He regarded Trisna. "Can you hold out a couple of minutes?"

"You're suddenly worried about me?" Trisna said.

"How about it, Doc?" Everett said. "Will a little wait hurt her worse?"

"She should be all right," Katla said. "But hurry."

"You got it."

Everett patted Pasco on the shoulder and they ran to the stairwell.

Katla became conscious of how vulnerable she and the other woman were there alone. "Let's hope no Martians wander by."

"I wouldn't blame them if they attacked us," Trisna said.

"That's crazy talk."

Trisna shifted and grunted. "Look at this from their point of view. We're the invaders, not them. Mars is their planet."

That's no excuse, was on the tip of Katla's tongue but she didn't say it. Trisna was right. Were the situation reversed, the military would do everything in its power to wipe out every last Martian.

"I tell you," Trisna said, "if we survive this, Behula and I are going back to Earth."

Katla remembered Archard saying there were thousands of creatures deep under the volcano. An entire city, was how he'd put it. And that might just be the tip of the Martian iceberg. "We all might have to."

47

Locked together, Archard and the blue Martian grappled fiercely. The RAM's gyro alarm warned that the battle suit was tumbling out of control.

Their titanic efforts spun them and flipped them, so that one moment Archard was on top, the next the blue Martian was above him.

Archard rammed a knee against the creature's abdomen, thinking it might be a weak spot, but its belly was protected by thick carapace. Archard pushed with all the RAM's strength. The creature wouldn't let go. It continued to apply pressure to the RAM's wrists.

A red light appeared. A new warning that the RAM was in danger of losing its airtight seal. The armor over both wrists had developed minute hairline fractures. If the Martian cracked them open, his internal atmosphere would be sucked out and he would die a horrible death.

No living thing could be that strong. Yet his suit's alarm proved otherwise.

Archard needed to gain the upper hand, and quickly. He kicked in the thrusters again and righted himself. Their descent slowed. Bending his hand down as far as it would go, Archard said, "Eat this!" and fired a dart into the thing's face.

At point-blank range, the razor-sharp flechettes tore through whatever vital organs its hulking body possessed.

The blue Martian went rigid. Its eye stalks drooped, its tail curled. Those formidable grippers relaxed, and at last it released him. Gravity took over, and down it plummeted.

Breathing heavily from his exertion, Archard watched until the creature was a blue speck far below. He would dearly love to follow it, to uncover the full extent of the Martians' civilization, but there were people in New Meridian counting on him to make it back alive.

By now every archway, bridge and thoroughfare overflowed with Martians. He swore he could feel hostility radiating from them like a palpable force.

Staying well clear of the walkways and bridges, Archard rose. A check showed that the RAM's structural integrity was intact, and all weapons systems were functional.

Another of the unusual yellow Martians with a bowl-shaped head appeared on a crowded archway.

Almost immediately a new sensation came over him, nausea so intense, he was almost sick. His consciousness flickered, as if something were trying to smother it. His arms and legs began to tingle.

Instinctively, Archard knew the yellow Martian was to blame. He managed to raise his arm. "Nice try," he said, and fired a missile. At the blast, scores of creatures spilled from the shattered archway, the yellow Martian among them.

Deep in his mind, Archard imagined he heard an inhuman scream, but probably not.

Archard got down to business. He spiraled upward, choosing targets, an edifice here, an avenue there. Missiles, darts, grenades, the ion cannons, magnetic bombs, the flame thrower, he used everything in the RAM's arsenal. He blasted, he fried, he disintegrated. He killed and killed and killed some more.

Rising above their city, he assessed the devastation. The RAM had proven itself. Towers and spires and cliff dwellings lay in rubble. Walkways and spans, destroyed. Dead Martians, and parts of Martians, were everywhere.

"You brought this on yourselves," Archard said. He felt no regret. Not after the Zabinskis, and the attack on the colony.

Increasing the EDM drive, he accelerated toward the caldera opening far above.

The RAM acted up as soon as Archard cleared the volcano. All systems still read green but the thrusters sputtered every now and then. The power level showed the RAM at fifteen percent. Low, but not low enough to cause the sputtering. He would recharge in New Meridian and hopefully be good to go for the next phase.

He tried to get through to the colony but—big surprise—no one answered.

Weary to his marrow, he limped along, so to speak. Whenever the RAM sputtered, he tensed, dreading the worst, but the battle suit kept going.

Archard doubted his attack on Albor Tholus would end the conflict. The events of the past couple of days were more likely the beginning of a broader clash that would turn Mars into a battlefield.

If the Martians were anything like humans, they would want to retaliate. Not just at New Meridian but at Wellsville and Bradbury. It was imperative he get word to the other colonies.

He was a quarter of a kilometer out when his earphones crackled.

"...tain...hear...me?"

"Private Everett, is that you?" Archard quickly responded. "I read you, but you're breaking up."

"Sir..." Everett said, and added more that came through in snatches.

"You're breaking up," Archard repeated. "Say again?"

Abruptly, electronic manna from heaven, their connection cleared.

"Sir, we've completed our sweep. We checked all the buildings and didn't find anyone else."

"Not a single soul?"

"No, sir. We found a lot of bodies and arms and legs. But the thing is, some are missing."

"How's that again?" Archard thought the Kentuckian was referring to their heads.

"Some of the houses have holes in the floors so we know the Martians were there. But there weren't any bodies. No blood, nothing. Dr. Dkany thinks they were taken captive."

Archard swore. "How many?

"No way to be sure. I'd guess up to thirty personnel."

There was nothing Archard could do. Given the vastness of the Martian underground, he'd need a small army to ferret the captives out. For now, he must concentrate on the few he could save. "Are the spare power cells charged?'

"Yes, sir. Everything is as you wanted. Extra food. Extra water. Extra ammo. The tank will be crammed."

"Can't be helped," Archard said. "Put some soup on. I want to head out as soon as possible."

"You must be hungry enough to eat a Martian," Everett quipped.

"Put out food for all of us," Archard said. "A last meal to tide us over."

"Got you," Everett said, and clicked off.

Since reception had been so clear, Archard tried to raise the other colonies. He should have known better.

At night, the dome's golden sheen was more of a dull bronze. Everything seemed peaceful until Archard was close enough to see through the tint. The Broadcast Center roof was a shambles. The Administrative Center had a large hole in the rear wall. Other buildings had also sustained damage. Torsos and legs sprinkled the streets.

Archard was glad to finally land. He clunked through the main airlock to find Katla and Private Pasco waiting. "You should have stayed at headquarters."

"Dr. Dkany wanted to come," Pasco said, "and Everett said she shouldn't do it alone so I came with her."

"Such a gallant gentleman you are," Katla said.

Archard had to grin when the young Spaniard blushed. "What's the latest?"

"We haven't seen any sign of the Martians since you lured them away," Katla said.

"They'll be back," Archard declared with absolute conviction.

"Let's hope we're long gone by then, sir," Private Pasco said.

"I hear that," Archard said.

48

Only when he had climbed out of the RAM did Archard appreciate how close he had come. The armor was dented and scratched all over. Some of the dents went in over a centimeter. Where the blue creature had gripped the suit's forearms were deep grooves.

Repair and recharging would take the better part of an hour.

Archard was annoyed by the delay but it couldn't be helped. The RAM must be in top shape. Their lives depended on it.

They ate quickly. The others were curious about the volcano so he gave them an abbreviated version.

"We've sure been lucky," Pasco said at the end.

"How do you figure?" Everett said.

"That blue thing the captain fought," Pasco said. "What if an army of them had attacked New Meridian instead of the smaller ones?"

"They still might," Everett said.

Archard saw to rearming the RAM personally. Perched on a ladder, he was sliding a magazine into an aperture in the housing when a hand touched his foot.

"I'm happy you made it back safe," Katla said.

"Makes two of us."

"We're taking a terrible gamble."

"Less than if we stay."

"Do you really believe we'll make it?"

Archard stopped working. "It's twelve hundred kilometers to Wellsville. The tank's range with a full charge is eight hundred. Loaded down as we're going to be, I'd reduce that to seven. Which leaves us five hundred kilometers short."

"All we have to do is recharge," Katla pointed out. "That's what the solar collectors are for."

"Recharging can take a full day. Longer, if the sky isn't clear. A delay we can't afford if the Martians come after us."

"Ah," Katla said.

Archard patted the RAM. "At low power, I can push the tank all day and all night without depleting the suit's reserves."

"Or the tank's."

"Exactly. I'll push you halfway there, and the tank can make the rest of the trip under its own power. With me keeping guard."

"Our protector," Katla said. "What happens once we get there? What will Governor Blanchard do? Order the planet abandoned?"

"Hardly. Earth's governments have too much invested. Their only recourse is to send up more troops."

"All-out war?" Katla shuddered.

Archard climbed down and took her in his arms. "I won't let anything happen to you."

"It's not that. It's the killing. I thought we had outgrown barbarism."

"What's barbaric about defending ourselves?" Archard countered. "We didn't start this."

"An honest-to-God war of the worlds," Katla said sadly.

Archard tried to lighten her mood with, "They don't call it the Red Planet for nothing."

Katla groaned.

Two hours later, they were underway.

Snug in the RAM, Archard waited for the tank to drive through the main airlock. He gazed at New Meridian for what might be the last time. An eerie stillness prevailed. He felt a profound sense of guilt at abandoning the colony he was supposed to protect. Were he the last man standing, he'd be tempted to stay and defend it with his dying breath. But he wasn't. Six other lives were at stake, to say nothing of the hundreds of colonists at Wellsville and Bradbury.

Archard had to stoop to enter the airlock, the RAM was so big. "All set, sir," his helmet crackled as he emerged.

Private Everett had turned off the tank and put it in neutral.

"Here we go." Archard placed the RAM's armored hands flat against the rear of the tank, and pushed. It was ridiculously easy. No strain whatsoever. "I leave the steering to you. Try not to hit anything."

"I won't, sir. But I can't promise Pasco won't when it's his turn to drive."

"Hey," Pasco said.

Tires crunching, the tank crawled forward across the vast Martian terrain.

Archard had little doubt they would reach Wellsville. Word would be relayed to Earth, and reinforcements would be sent. He imagined an entire battalion, with half-a dozen RAM's. Then it would be Earth's turn to unleash devastating payback.

Look out, Martians. Here we come.

FINI

David Robbins is the author of over three hundred published novels including the internationally famous ENDWORLD series and the new ANGEL U series. Some of his other works include The WILDERNESS series and the novelizations of the films PROOF OF LIFE (Staring Russell Crowe) and MEN OF HONOR (Staring Robert De Niro). His books have been translated into nine languages and sold millions of copies worldwide. He is a member of the Horror Writers Association and the Science Fiction and Fantasy Writers of America.

Made in the USA
Middletown, DE
12 April 2016